Fangs, Frost, and Folios

Giovanni and Beatrice left vampire conspiracies and supernatural adventures for a peaceful family life. But peace only lasts so long for a vampire assassin and an undying scribe.

The death of an old friend leaves Giovanni with a rare opportunity. He knows that Lady Penelope's library hides more than one rare book, but can he break into her family's ancestral home without raising the alarm? Giovanni and Beatrice are looking for literary treasure. Other lurking immortals might be searching for a different and more dangerous haul.

Back in Los Angeles, Ben and Tenzin were put in charge of protecting the family. But can two powerful vampires survive the mercurial mood swings of a preteen girl? Ben and Tenzin could be facing the end... of their sanity.

Fangs, Frost, and Folios is a holiday novella and a brand-new adventure for Giovanni and Beatrice, the heroes of the Elemental Mysteries series by eleven-time *USA Today* best-selling author Elizabeth Hunter.

Fangs, Frost, and Folios

An Elemental Mysteries Novella

Elemental Mysteries
Book Six

Elizabeth Hunter

Let us once lose our oaths to find ourselves,
Or else we lose ourselves to keep our oaths.

— Love's Labour's Lost, William
Shakespeare

ONE

Giovanni Vecchio, centuries-old fire vampire, former assassin, wealthy collector, and the immortal world's foremost literary researcher, picked up the tweezers he was using to build a model ship and promptly dropped them.

"What am I doing?" He stared at the miniature galleon in pieces on his study table. Hundreds of wooden parts that he would spend hours assembling so he could put the finished model on a shelf to collect dust with the half dozen other models he'd completed over the past month.

What was next? A model-train room?

He stood and eyed the tweezers on the desk. "Absolutely not."

It had to stop. He liked a quiet life. He'd fought battles to attain this life and the safety it provided for his mate and his children.

But there was safe, and there was boring.

"Beatrice!" He stood in the study, staring at the fire with his hands on his hips.

It had been her idea to take on more vampire clients, and he'd foolishly dismissed her.

"I should have known," he muttered.

His mate was blood bound to him; at times he thought she knew him better than he knew himself. Beatrice must have sensed he was getting restless.

"Giovanni?"

He turned to see Caspar in the doorway. "Cas. I didn't mean to bother you. Is Beatrice busy?"

"She's currently involved in a very delicate political negotiation."

He glanced at the clock. "Sadia."

"Indeed. It's no easy feat trying to convince your daughter that having vampire parents does not mean vampire hours for the human child." The older man smiled. "If I recall correctly, I tried something similar at her age."

"I remember." Giovanni remembered everything, and it would eventually devastate him. His oldest child was aging. Caspar's steel-grey hair was turning to pure white. His shoulders were stooped and he moved slowly. He was in his late eighties now, and Giovanni knew he wouldn't live another decade.

Part of him understood Sadia's resistance to sleep. Time was precious indeed.

Caspar's eyes lit up. "I see you've started on the galleon. Is there anything I can help with? Isadora is already sleeping, so I feel quite useless at the moment."

"I can relate to that."

The old man's eyes sparkled. "Is that so?"

Giovanni walked to the bar to pour two glasses of the whiskey they both enjoyed, motioning Caspar to take a seat by the fire. "You told me she was right."

"She usually is." He lowered himself into a wingback chair angled toward the fire.

There were always vampires who wanted his and his wife's expertise to find lost correspondence hidden away in a library, pilfered personal journals, or a rare edition of a book that had been out of print for two hundred years.

Giovanni had argued that their lives were full. They didn't need to work, so why not spend their time with the daughter they'd adopted a decade ago? Childhood sped by too quickly; he knew that from raising two other children.

Giovanni passed Caspar a glass of whiskey and sat across from him. "You handed me two letters the other day. Both of them could be interesting. Model-ship building?" He shook his head. "I'll turn into a statue like the immortals of Alitea."

"One letter was from a vampire lord in Benin, and the other was from an associate of Carwyn's in Colombia." Caspar sipped the whiskey in his glass. "But I might have a job closer to home if you're looking for something... intriguing."

"Oh?" Giovanni stretched out his long legs, his eyes on the fire in the grate. He reached out, drawing it toward him and then pushing it back, pulsing the heat into the room. Los Angeles didn't get as cold as other parts of the world, but it was the middle of December and the great old house in San Marino carried a damp chill. "I don't know if I want closer to home. I believe I could use a departure from the ordinary."

"This might serve. Do you remember Lady Penelope Percy-Reed?"

"Speaking of 'out of the ordinary.'" Giovanni smiled. "Plucky Penny Reed? Hostess to the wildest country parties in the earl's ancestral heap? Of course I remember Penny. Damn, I'd forgotten the two of you still corresponded. Much longer friendship than the original romance, I think."

Caspar smiled. "She happily married Mortimer in nineteen sixty-eight."

Giovanni muttered, "When he was sixty-eight himself if I remember correctly."

"Not nearly. Forties at most." Caspar shrugged. "Maybe fifties. He made her happy."

"That's the point then, isn't it?"

Lady Penelope Percy-Reed had come from one of those venerable families who all married each other in the English countryside, keeping the wealth concentrated over the centuries. Caspar had been a student and the adopted son of a fire vampire, which meant absolutely nothing in English society. However Lady Penny might have admired the handsome young student who courted her, it would never have worked out in the long run.

Nevertheless, Penny was a bohemian, an artist, and a brash young thing who smoked and drank like a man of her time, drove too fast in her father's sports cars, rode horses, took flying lessons, loved dogs of all kinds, and filled her weekend house parties with interesting people who had no money of their own. She was a patron of the arts, a consumer of good brandy, and a lifelong friend.

She had become a lady of the manor married to Lord Mortimer, an Englishman of ancient lineage and a man of considerable wealth, but Giovanni suspected she had never lost her verve.

"How is Penny these days?"

Caspar's smile was soft. "Her great-nephew said she was very peaceful at the end."

"Oh Caspar." Giovanni's heart sank. "I'm so sorry."

"It seems most letters I get these days come from either heirs or lawyers." He pulled a folded envelope out of his cardigan pocket. "She passed a little over a week ago. Heart condition. She'd been on medication for years; it wasn't a surprise."

"We're never prepared to lose a friend."

Caspar nodded and sipped his drink.

Giovanni tried not to let the silence stretch. "Where was she?"

"Hereford. She and Mortimer moved out to his country estate nearly forty years ago. Old Morty had a brother there, and they were close. They were quite involved with their niece and nephews and their education. The brother passed away when the children were quite young. A number of great-nieces and nephews in the new generation. Good family."

"And one of them was with her at the end?" Giovanni nodded. "I'm glad."

"As am I. She spoke very highly of the young man. He's the oldest of the lot. Nicholas, I believe his name is. He's a musician and a primary schoolteacher in the village."

"And the twelfth something or other of Herefordshire?"

Caspar shrugged. "All that as well since the title passed from his uncle. They never had children of their own, so Penny was always quite glad that the children were active, useful sorts."

"A good life then." Giovanni raised his glass. "To Plucky Penny. A magnificent woman and a well-lived life."

"To Penny." Caspar lifted his own glass and took a sip. "Now, about Penny and Mortimer's old library..."

Beatrice De Novo shut her daughter's bedroom door, pretending she didn't hear the indignant huff on the other side. Her fangs dropped instinctively as she turned to Dema, Sadia's nanny and bodyguard.

"Military academy?" She took two careful steps from the door. "Do they have those for girls?"

"Absolutely." Dema had been in the military herself, and she didn't blink. "I can look up options tomorrow." The woman's face was implacable, her even features revealing neither amusement nor disapproval.

"No." Beatrice closed her eyes and forced her fangs

back. "It's a phase. She'll grow out of this at some point, and I'll have my delightful and wonderful child back. This is just..."

"Twelve."

"Twelve." Beatrice sighed. "Tell me it gets better."

"It gets better. You don't remember being that age?" Dema shrugged. "Everything is a drama."

They walked down the hall and toward the stairs. "You'd think I'd told her she had to cut off her hair and wear sackcloth instead of pick out her clothes for school tomorrow and go to bed."

"B, don't you know how she suffers?" Dema was already looking at her mobile device. "I'm logging into the captive portal, so she won't have Wi-Fi in a minute."

"Just make sure you tell Giovanni this time." Her husband was accomplished in many things, but technology was not one of them. "Last night he was trying to look at something on YouTube, and he—"

"Beatrice!" The vampire in question walked from his study into the living room. "We have a job."

Dema and Beatrice shared a knowing look.

"What kind of job?" Beatrice asked.

"Not putting tiny ships together." He reached for her hand over the banister. "I see the look, Dema. There will be no more models. Please tell Zain to take them away."

"Thank God," Dema muttered. "Tell me some country lost a national archive or something."

"That might be more work than we want, but I do know of a missing play."

Beatrice's eyebrows went up. Her mate was a dark

and dangerous fire vampire, a sixteenth-century assassin, and a meticulous scholar. He could also be incredibly charming when he wanted to be.

"A missing play? I'm listening."

"A play." Giovanni led her toward the living room, where a fire was already burning. "By someone you might have heard of before."

Beatrice's librarian blood was humming. "And that would be...?"

"A lost comedy by the Bard himself." Giovanni led her toward a chaise and waited for her to sit before he bowed over her hand and kissed her knuckles. "*Love's Labour's Won.*"

"You're not serious." Beatrice blinked. "Do you mean—?"

"How would you like to go to the English countryside for Christmas so we can search a vast aristocratic library for something that may or may not exist?"

"If it's a lost Shakespeare play, yes!" Beatrice felt as if she'd resurfaced from drowning. "Absolutely yes!"

His deep green eyes were dancing. "I was hoping you'd say that. The library belonged to Lady Penelope Percy-Reed, an old friend of Caspar's." He paced in front of the fire.

Beatrice was delighted by his excitement. "How did she end up getting—?"

"Allegedly."

"An unpublished Shakespeare play?"

"Allegedly," Dema added.

"Indeed allegedly." Giovanni's lips quirked. "Penny's

great-great-something or other was an actress if family rumors are to be believed."

"An actress? *Scandalous*." Beatrice's heart began to race.

"This was during Shakespeare's time?" Dema perched on the back of a long couch. "I thought women weren't allowed to act then."

"According to Penny, her ancestor was a noblewoman who disguised herself as a young man so she could act the women's parts on the stage."

"No." Beatrice grinned. "Are you kidding? That's amazing."

"Appalling family rumors are the only proof, of course." Giovanni slid next to Beatrice and took her hand. "But the delicious rumor was backed up—according to Penny—by the possession of an *unfinished* play given to her ancestor by Shakespeare himself."

"*Love's Labour's Won*?" The sequel to Shakespeare's famous comedy had long been rumored, but Beatrice hadn't found any theories to be convincing.

"I honestly don't know." He leaned back. "Penny was always vague when she brought it up. It's possible she fabricated the entire story—she never let facts get in the way of good fiction—but her great-nephew just sent Caspar a letter letting him know that Penelope had passed and that he expected to find various bequests to friends when the solicitors finished their inventory of the library."

Beatrice cocked her head. "Is that standard?"

"To inventory a family library? Not typical, but not

unheard of. Particularly when parts of the library are being designated to various institutions for preservation. It's convenient for us though. The lawyers are coming after the holiday." Giovanni smiled. "My plane can get us there faster."

"We can pose as experts working for the solicitor's office."

"An easy enough ruse, particularly for you."

Beatrice looked up the stairs. "Would we be gone for Christmas? Sadia is driving me crazy right now, but I don't want to abandon our child on her holiday break."

He frowned. "Why not?"

"Gio."

"If we leave, she might find enough grace in her twelve-year-old heart to miss us."

Beatrice knew he was speaking from experience. He'd raised two boys to adulthood, and neither had cut him off or gone to jail.

At least not for any length of time.

"I think if we're efficient, we'll be back in time for the holiday." Giovanni rubbed her back. "But, of course, she will be finished with school next week." He looked at Dema. "Any plans for the holidays we should know about?"

Dema squinted. "As I don't celebrate Christmas except in the secular way that everyone in this country celebrates the red-coated festival of capitalism, you know I will be around. Also, I believe Zain told me he was visiting family at the New Year, not on Christmas."

"And we all know that Zain is the only person Sadia listens to these days," Giovanni said. "This is perfect."

Their house manager was in his late twenties and the only "cool" person in the house according to their twelve-year-old. Dema was a nagging older sister who worried too much. Her parents were clueless, of course, despite the literal centuries of collective life experience they had accumulated.

"I have an idea," Dema said. "You two go to England to look for the lost book—"

"Play."

Beatrice cocked her head. "Folio, perhaps?"

Dema sighed. "All the book nerds go to England. Sadia stays here with me and Zain, and you call Ben and Tenzin so they can spend the holidays with her and she'll have family around if you two get delayed for any reason."

Beatrice looked at Giovanni. Her husband was nodding his approval.

Adventure. Intrigue. Dusty stacks and hidden corners.

Beatrice felt her blood start to move.

"When do we leave?"

Tenzin stared at her wall of swords, contemplating where to put the new one she'd ordered for herself from her dealer in San Francisco. It was a seventeenth-century Indo-Persian short sword with a jeweled inlay on the handle, and she had lost a similar weapon two centuries before.

Did she need another sword?

That was an idiotic question. Of course she needed more swords.

Ben walked into the living area of the loft with a green bird perched on his shoulder. "Did you let the birds in the house?"

Tenzin blinked and opened her eyes wide. "No."

Layah and Harun had been staring at her in the roof garden, loudly chirping and letting her know they did not approve of the winter weather and overcast skies despite their well-heated tropical enclosure.

Tenzin had let them jump onto her shoulder in a moment of weakness. She hadn't really *let* them into the house. They just kind of followed her, and she didn't stop them.

Ben leaned against the doorframe. "So a stranger went up to the roof garden, let them out of their enclosure, and brought them down to the apartment?"

"Maybe they broke out and came to find us because they missed us."

He closed his eyes. "There's bird shit on your armor in the hallway."

Her jaw dropped and she glared at Harun. "Betrayer! You swore you'd behave yourself." Her head whipped back to Ben. "The Japanese armor or the Czech?"

"The one that looks like a scary-as-shit statue with a rabbit on its head."

"The Japanese." She narrowed her eyes at Harun.

"Where is Layah? Is she shitting on any of my other possessions?"

"In the birds' defense, the armor does look a lot like a statue."

Just then a bright yellow flicker chirped overhead, Harun took off to follow his mate, who had been perched on Tenzin's German short sword, and a plop of white bird poop fell to the floor.

Ben looked at her. "You're cleaning it up."

She wrinkled her nose. "Why don't we have servants here?"

"Because we're capable of cleaning up after ourselves." He glanced up. "And our pets."

Tenzin glowered. *Speak for yourself.*

He walked to the kitchen, leaving Tenzin on the floor, still staring up at the sword wall. She didn't want to think about bird poop, so she thought about swords and other shiny things. "I ordered myself a saber for Christmas."

Ben's beautiful mouth curved into a smile, and Tenzin was reminded again how happy she was that she hadn't killed him any of the many times he'd annoyed her.

"I think you're still struggling with the idea of how Christmas presents work."

"Don't say that when I was just thinking how happy I am that I didn't kill you."

Ben blinked. "What?"

"I got you a sword too. And a map of Australia from the eighteenth century. It's horribly inaccurate."

"That's not the point of collecting historic maps, and

can we go back to you being happy you didn't kill me? When was this?"

"Various times over the years. Not since we've been... you know."

"Mated vampires?" He leaned over the counter. "*Mates*. Not in the friendly Australian way, but the kind that shag—if we're keeping to the Aussie vernacular."

He always sounded so smug when he said it.

"Yes, that." Tenzin glanced at the ruby ring on her left hand. "And I don't know if your Australian slang is accurate, Benjamin."

He clearly didn't care. "When are you getting me a ring?"

"I got you a map of Australia." She rolled her eyes. "That's much better."

"I want a ring."

"We're not married."

"I didn't ask to get married. I want a ring, and I know you have a thousand of them hidden away in various caches. Pick one for me and I'll wear it."

"Why?" She flipped upside down and floated. Maybe she'd get a better idea of the wall layout from another angle.

"Because I asked you."

She already had a ring picked out for him. It was a triple gold band from a cache of gold she'd found in Scotland. She just didn't want him to make a big deal about it.

Emotions were tricky, and she was still sorting through them. She'd taken deliberate steps to expand her emotional range, but it didn't come easy after five millennia. Ben's emotions were quicksilver—excited to happy to furious to merry in moments that flashed like moving pictures.

Tenzin preferred.

To think.

Ben had already moved on to a new subject. "My uncle just called me. How would you feel about going to California for Christmas this year?"

"We can do that. It will be warmer." She glanced at the birds, who were grooming themselves on a fifth-century Indian dagger. "Can we take the birds with us?"

Ben pursed his lips. "You know, I feel like Arthur and Drew would be unhappy if we didn't ask them to housesit and take care of the kids."

"Arthur and Drew like our loft and our roof garden. And our proximity to the theater district during the holiday season."

"And us."

She sighed. "Layah and Harun don't like their dogs."

"I don't think Layah and Harun have even met their dogs." He walked over and floated until he was face-to-face with her. "Gio and B are going to England for a job. They want us to go stay with Sadia so she's not alone. On the off chance they get delayed, they don't want her without family on Christmas."

A holiday in Los Angeles with Ben's diabolical little sister all to herself?

Tenzin smiled. "We can leave tomorrow night."

Two

They landed at Stansted Airport north of London just before dusk, two nights after Giovanni threw away the model ship. He hadn't spared a minute before communicating with Gemma Melcombe, the earth vampire who ruled London with her mate and husband Terrance Ramsay.

The vampire world was one of warlords, territories, and courts built on favor and favors. Humans might see it as medieval, but it kept the peace among highly competitive predators. Seeking permission to work in a vampire's territory was often perfunctory, but it prevented competing interests from clashing in front of a mortal audience.

Since they were old friends, working in Gemma's territory was never an issue, and Giovanni maintained a country house in Kent that he rented out to oblivious humans when he wasn't using it.

Beatrice was already awake when he roused from his

day-sleep. She'd inherited the strange quirk of day-walking from her sire, so while she found a few hours of rest in the middle of the day, she had hours to spend reading and passing time while the sun ruled.

He opened his eyes and saw her sitting in the lounge chair across from the bed where she usually read when they were flying. Her hair was undone, spilling over her shoulders in rippling waves from the braid she'd worn the night before. Her hair was dark brown, nearly black, and her skin was pale with olive undertones bestowed by her human blood.

Her deep brown eyes warmed when she saw he was awake. "Good evening, husband."

Giovanni leaped out of the bed like the predator he was and pounced on her, caging her on the lounge chair as he bent down and inhaled a deep breath at the curve of her neck. She smelled of honey and something citrus that lingered on her skin.

"I already took my shower for the night." She put her hands on his chest. "You're naked."

"I hate sleeping in clothes."

"Oh, that's right, you do." Her hand ran from his chest, down his abdomen, and closed around the erection that was more than wide-awake. "Is this for me?"

"Always." He ran his fangs along her neck. "You're wearing clothes."

"We've been parked in a hangar for two hours. I took a shower and got dressed to pass the time."

"We pay the staff well; they can wait for us." He slid off the chair and down to his knees in front of Beatrice, his fangs slicing open her neat grey button-front shirt. "I'll buy you a new one."

"Yes, you will." She slid off the wrecked garment and immediately rid herself of the hateful underthings that were blocking Giovanni from seeing her body. "Someone is in a mood."

"I'm feeling festive." He looked around. "I'll need to find some mistletoe to carry around with me." He tugged off her slim black pants and picked her up, then walked the few short steps to the bed and tossed her on the mattress.

Beatrice propped herself up on her elbows. "You know the use of mistletoe is a remnant of pre-Christian druidic practices associated with male virility."

"Even more reason to carry some around." He lifted her leg, peppering kisses along the curve of her calf, the back of her knee, and up the inside of her thigh. "Male virility, you say?"

She lifted her other foot and slid one toe up the underside of his erection. "Not really something you need to think about."

"Vixen." He grinned and dropped her leg, covering her body with his own, taking her mouth in a greedy kiss and sliding between her thighs until he was seated to the hilt.

They rocked together in lazy loving, laughing and rolling in the sheets until Beatrice's back arched in ecstasy and Giovanni chased her climax with a burst of furious pleasure. He felt flames rise on his back, but his mate drew water to his skin, cooling it and soothing the ache before it could take root in his flesh. Steam filled their stateroom and enveloped them in a warm cocoon.

Burning was one of the few harms that could befall an immortal. To die, they had to burn or lose their heads.

Giovanni only lost his head metaphorically in the presence of his wife.

"I love you." He lay on his back, drawing her head to his chest and playing with the ends of her hair. "Life with you is like an extended holiday."

She burrowed her face in his chest. "We're very lucky."

"We are." The scope of their challenge jumped to the forefront of his mind. "How long do we have before Christmas?"

"Fourteen days."

"Fourteen days." He nodded. "We'd probably better start the drive out to Hereford. Gemma found a house for us, but it's a three-hour drive from London and even longer from the house in Kent."

"So you called Gemma?"

Giovanni smiled. "She's very happily married to Terry now. No lingering feelings for this old vampire."

"She still flirts with you."

"Only to make Terry jealous."

"I'm going to stab her one of these days. Not anywhere fatal, just somewhere painful."

He sat up, pulling Beatrice onto his lap. "I do love when you get jealous and violent."

"Just don't tell our impressionable daughter." She

brushed his hair back from his forehead. "I'm supposed to be setting a good example."

"Good examples are highly overrated among the twelve-year-old set," he said. "More bad examples are warranted, I think. She's probably far too safe for her own good."

"Remember when Ben got death threats when he was fourteen?"

Giovanni sighed. "Yes."

"Tenzin is with her," Beatrice said. "Nothing will happen when Tenzin is with her, and if there's anyone who can set a bad example for her—"

"It's Tenzin."

"Exactly." Beatrice rested her chin on Giovanni's shoulder. "Okay, let's get dressed and go drive in the mud. Did your ex-girlfriend at least get us a good car?"

"If by good car you mean a 1983 Range Rover with crank windows and dodgy heating, then yes. Absolutely."

The drive to Hereford in a manual-transmission Range Rover was bumpy, muddy once they got off the main road, and twisting. Beatrice had never been to Herefordshire, and she'd never been to rural England at Christmas.

She'd enjoyed the lights and festive decorations she'd seen as they drove through the village. There were brightly decorated trees and holly wreaths along with a light dusting of snow that reflected the moonlight and brightened the night.

She tried not to feel guilty that they were seeing all these charming things and beautiful scenery without Sadia and Ben but reminded herself that Ben was a grown man and had an immortal lifetime of travel in front of him, and Sadia was a preteen who was only interested in what her friends were interested in. Lately that meant graphic novels, vintage concert T-shirts from bands Beatrice had listened to in high school, and LED lights stuck all over her room.

And swords. She did love a good blade, and Beatrice was proud of that.

"Do you think Tenzin and Ben are in LA yet?"

"They usually take three days to fly unless they're in a rush." Giovanni navigated a narrow stone bridge and wound the Range Rover through the hedgerows past Hereford town. "Probably tomorrow night."

"She'll be happy when they get there," Beatrice said. "She always loves it when they visit."

"Sadia is fine," he said. "She'll hardly miss us."

But what if I miss her?

Beatrice shook her head and tried to focus. She'd been in mother mode for too long. She needed a challenge that she could actually solve, and snooping through an old library for a couple of weeks sounded perfect. "Did you contact the nephew yet?"

"I had our butler in Kent call him. He said the young man seemed overly agreeable and completely cooperative.

I don't think I'll even have to use amnis to get in the house."

People, on average, were remarkably trusting of anyone with a friendly voice, a briefcase, and a clipboard. Beatrice had brought all three. "I brought my old staff ID from the Huntington."

"Excellent."

They crossed another narrow stone bridge, passed a large hunting cottage on the edge of the woods, and followed the one-way track into the trees. The road turned from pavement to gravel, and Giovanni slowed the car.

In the distance, Beatrice saw a brown stone manor house, its black slate roof rising from the mist. Around it was a stone wall that matched the great house with a heavy iron gate, a guardhouse on the right.

A man in a navy peacoat stepped out of the guardhouse. He had a military bearing and an earpiece. "Can I help you, sir?"

"We're expected," Giovanni said. "Vecchio and De Novo."

"Of course, sir. Give me one moment."

The man walked around the car, speaking quietly into a communication device at his wrist. Within moments, he was back. He nodded at Giovanni and tapped the side of the Range Rover, his breath frosting in the chilly air. "You've checked out, Mr. Vecchio. Lord Ramsay welcomes you to Graves Court."

"Thank you." The gates opened, and Giovanni pulled forward.

"Graves Court?" Beatrice asked. "Do we need to be worried?"

He smiled. "I believe Terry bought this around a century ago. The name is more dire than the edifice."

The edifice was, in fact, a Tudor-style manor house with a steep roof and a distinct lack of holiday lights. In a nod to hospitality, there was a large Christmas tree in one window and staff waiting at the front door.

"Secure," Beatrice murmured. "With Terry, you know it will be secure."

"Some of us pass out completely during daylight." Her husband smiled. "Not that there's much of it this time of year."

Days were short in the winter, and the air was frigid when a dark-jacketed servant opened Beatrice's car door.

"Ms. De Novo and Mr. Vecchio," he said. "Welcome to Graves Court."

Ben landed in the backyard of the house in San Marino, expecting to see his little sister jumping on the trampoline or riding her bike in the courtyard. She would drop everything and run to him, thrilled he was visiting after six months away.

"Hmm." Tenzin dropped down next to him and looked around. "I like the new arbor."

"What?" Ben looked around and saw a mission-style

redwood arbor where the trampoline used to sit. "What happened to the trampoline?"

"I suspect your sister doesn't use it anymore." Tenzin waved at someone in the distance. "Dema has spotted us."

Ben looked around the house in confusion. "Did they go out? I told you we needed to call them before we got here."

Tenzin lifted her face and took a deep breath. "Sadia is here. I can smell her."

Ben frowned. "It's strange when you do that. Please don't do that."

"If you paid attention, you'd be able to smell her too. She smells like—"

"Nope." He raised a hand and walked toward Dema. "We are not talking about the way my little sister smells. That's a level of vampire weird I'm just not comfortable with yet."

Dema smiled as she approached. "Hey, guys. Good to see you. Zain made up the guesthouse. I figured that's where you'd want to be."

"Sure, thanks." Ben bent down and hugged Sadia's nanny, who was practically a member of the family at this point. Not that she didn't have her own family too. "How's your mom and dad?"

"Good. Busy. Don Ernesto is having some big holiday party, and my mom is helping plan it for all the employees. It's all she can think about right now, so I'm just glad I don't have to live with her."

"You're Muslim." Tenzin pursed her lips. "I assume your mother is too."

Dema was used to Tenzin's bluntness. "She is. This is a holiday party for all faiths, so that's what she's planning."

Tenzin frowned. "But it will be mostly Christmas themed because Ernesto is Christian."

Ben put his arm around Tenzin. "Everyone loves a party, Tiny. Just go with it." He looked around the house. "Where's Sadia?"

"In her room listening to Pearl Jam on a cassette player she found at a thrift shop last week." Dema bit back a smile. "She asked me if I'd ever heard of them before."

"What?" He frowned. "Who listens to cassette tapes anymore? That's even before my time."

"I have a collection of vinyl records somewhere." Tenzin gazed into the distance. "Marvelous technology, but still not as good as live music. What's a cassette tape? Is it sticky?"

Dema stared.

"There was a good fifty years or so that she just..." Ben waved a hand over Tenzin's head. "It's debatable whether it's worth catching her up or not."

The nanny smiled. "Well, good news. Sadia knows everything about Pearl Jam, cassette tapes, and grunge music, so if Tenzin wants to know, she's come to the right place."

Tenzin and Dema exchanged a look that Ben couldn't interpret.

"Oh." Tenzin smiled. "So she's there?"

"Oh, she is *so* there." Dema rolled her eyes. "Hormones are raging."

Ben blinked. "What? Hormones? What are you...?" Realization dawned. "No."

"Ben, your sister is twelve now. She's almost a teenager," Dema said. "It's perfectly normal."

He rushed past them into the house. Not Sadia. Not his baby sister. She was far too young for all the teenage drama and tears and the—

"Ben?"

He saw her at the top of the stairs. "Hey! We just got here. Dema was telling Tenzin that you're a Pearl Jam fan now. Did you know I saw them in Chicago when I was—?"

"Oh my God," she mumbled. "It's not, like, a big deal. I'm more into Green Day now." Sadia rolled her eyes beneath overlong black bangs, huffed out a breath, and spun around. "Welcome home or... whatever since you don't live here anymore. Mom and Dad went to look for some old stuff in London or something. Sorry you had to waste your time to come babysit me for Christmas."

Ben felt attacked, and he'd barely spoken a word. "Uh... hi? Happy to see you? How's it going? Missed you too?"

Sadia let out a long sigh. "Hey. I missed you and Tenzin even though we, like, talk every week. Why didn't you tell Mom and Dad I could go to New York with you guys?"

"Because we wanted to come to LA to see you?"

What was happening? Why was she angry? What was going on? "Are you okay?"

"I'm fine!" Sadia screwed up her face into an indignant expression. "Just..." She sighed deeply, rolled her eyes, and swept down the stairs past him. "Fine."

THREE

Audley Manor was a redbrick Jacobean mansion with soaring round towers framing a set of double doors painted bright green with gold trim. The giant cobbled courtyard was dusted with snow and lit by Christmas lights. A formal garden was bedded for the winter season, and wrought iron lampposts dotted the grounds.

Beatrice looked around as flakes of snow started to fall. "I feel like an owl is going to fly down at any moment and drop off an envelope with my invitation to wizarding school."

"Is that what you want for Christmas?" His wife was an endless amusement. "An owl?"

"No," she whispered. "I want a mystery."

He put his arm around her and pulled her close. "And I believe you'll have one."

Giovanni hadn't visited Penny after she moved to Herefordshire with her husband. He tried to imagine his bright human friend as the lady of this formal manor and had a hard time picturing it.

"Her house in Kent was nothing like this." He waited next to Beatrice as his wife rang the massive bell at the front door.

"What was her house in Kent like?"

"More of a well-loved pile. Old castle. Woods and meadows everywhere. A million dogs wandering around and run-down stables where she brewed homemade cider." He looked around, imagining the cost of upkeep and staff that a manor like Audley had to require. "Then again, it was probably falling apart at the seams. I always suspected that Penny married Mortimer for his money."

"You make her sound conniving."

"She wasn't. She was practical." Giovanni smiled. "She told me once that she could love anyone if she'd had enough gin."

Beatrice smiled. "She sounds like a character."

"And an imminently kind soul." He looked up at the stone crest over the door. "I'm sure she did love him. Penny could find something lovable about anyone. Even a vampire assassin."

Beatrice's face went blank. "Please tell me you were never hired to kill anyone she liked."

"Oh, I'd retired by the time I knew Penny." He cocked his head. "One or two of her ancestors however..."

"Gio."

"The Jacobean period was complicated. That's all I'll say."

The door opened to a stern-faced woman wearing a black uniform. "May I help you?"

"Giovanni Vecchio and Beatrice De Novo of Henrik Brothers, London. We're here to see Nicholas Mortimer. We were sent by the offices of Prescott and Bales Solicitors in London."

She opened the door wide. "We weren't expecting anyone this evening, but I'll let His Lordship know."

Nicholas Ralph Mortimer was an unassuming young man of thirty-one with a mop of wavy blond hair, cheerful blue eyes, and the wiles of a suburban golden retriever.

"Such a stroke of luck that Aunt Penny had friends in antiquarian-book circles," Nicholas said. "But not a surprise of course. I think Aunt Penny knew everyone. There was an absolute menagerie at her funeral; she would have loved it."

"I was privileged to meet Lady Penelope on multiple occasions and even attended a party or two at her family estate in Kent. Her loss cannot be overstated." Giovanni was shocked the young man hadn't asked to see a single credential, but it made life easier when humans were trusting. "It so happens that Beatrice and I have worked in curation and authentication for your aunt's solicitors on multiple occasions. You can depend on us for discretion and accuracy."

The young man waved a hand. "I've no doubt. I'm sure if they hired you that you are the best in your line of work." He smiled innocently. "I don't really know that much about Aunt Penny and Uncle Mort's book collection myself—just the children's section I'm afraid—though I do make frequent use of the modern-book corner Penny kept for guests." The young man smiled. "Love a good spy novel when I'm not working."

He was like a lamb. An innocent country lamb sitting on a giant pile of gold. Dear God, it was so tempting to rob him blind.

"You're a primary school teacher, I believe?"

"I am, and I also direct the orchestra at the secondary school in the village. Music is my passion, though I suspect I'll have to cut back on teaching a bit now." He looked around the house. "I always knew in the back of my mind that I'd be in charge of all this someday, but it's still sinking in."

Beatrice leaned forward, her button-down shirt gaping slightly at the neck. From the side, Giovanni could see the swell of her breast and the delicate fang marks he'd left on her when she was still mortal.

Focus.

"I hope our hours won't disturb you," his wife said. "Authentication is often a process that happens during business hours, but in a family home such as this—"

"It's fine. Really." He looked around the green salon where a fire burned in the grate and the house staff had decorated with tinsel and pine boughs for the holiday. "My fiancée and I—Elise, I'm sure you'll meet her when she's back from town—live on the grounds in the old dowager cottage at the moment." His eyes fell. "I suppose we'll be moving into the manor house eventually, but it all seems a bit overwhelming at the moment."

"Of course," Giovanni said. "We don't want to inconvenience you, especially around the holidays."

"Do you know if a catalog of the collection has ever been made?" Beatrice asked. "If we could work off an existing catalog, it might go faster."

"I don't think so. Penny always talked about hiring someone to do it, but then she also said that some of the collection should go back to Kent eventually, to her family home." The young man smiled with a hapless expression. "I'm really not sure what is what at this point. They were married for so many years."

"We'll do what we can with the records we can find," Beatrice said. "Did she ever talk about how the library was organized? If there was some kind of system in place for—"

"You know..." Nick stood and clapped his hands together. "Why don't I just show you in and let you" — he waved a hand— "do your magic. I'm quite the wrong person to ask at the end of the day. You'll probably have much better luck speaking to Barnes about it. He'll know."

"Barnes?" Beatrice leaned forward. "And Barnes is...?"

"The butler of course."

Giovanni's antennae immediately went up. "I see."

"He runs the house, and he worked for Uncle Mort

for years. If anyone knows how to answer your questions, it'll be him."

"Excellent." Giovanni smiled, but he wondered if Barnes might prove more of an obstacle than young Nick. After all, someone in the house had to be savvy. In his experience, servants were the brains behind the running of large estates, not the owners. "If you could show us to the library, and when Barnes is available—"

"He should be back tomorrow evening," Nick said. "He's visiting his daughter this weekend."

"Again, thank you so much for seeing us," Beatrice said. "I know it's Sunday night, but with a project like this, there's really no time to waste."

"Of course."

Beatrice stood in the doorway of the library at Audley Manor and stared. "This is the biggest private library—"

"Don't. You're going to offend me."

"The house in Perugia doesn't count because that's *only* a library." She wandered through the rows of bookshelves that stretched to the ceiling. "Perugia is a house for books that happens to have a couple of small dwellings for humans attached. This library is..."

"Impressive."

"Massive." Fourteen days would not be enough. "Giovanni" —she spun toward him— "can we buy it?"

"Do we have the money?" He shrugged. "I imagine you have enough currency in one of your play accounts to buy this place if you really wanted it."

"It's not a *play* account. It's an investment account. Just because I don't stack bars of gold in my closet doesn't mean my money isn't real."

"So you say." He walked down the central walkway. "This is far larger than I expected as well. I suspect Lord Mortimer's family might have more than one valuable in this old place." His eyes gleamed. "Maybe we *should* make an offer."

Beatrice saw a cozy nook by a fireplace in the corner where a piano was nestled among overstuffed chairs, a few wingbacks, and several well-loved sofas. It did appear that the room was well used, and the spy novels Nick had spoken of were lined up on shelves above rows of picture books and puzzles.

She smiled at the signs of life and love. "Despite our literary greed, I have a feeling that the new earl—while not fully embracing his role—might not be willing to part with a house with this much family history."

Giovanni was staring above the mantel to where a large portrait hung. "There she is." He smiled. "Good old Plucky Penny."

Beatrice looked up to see a woman with laughing grey eyes and soft brown hair. She was a classic English beauty with an oval face and a gentle smile. Standing at her shoulder was a barrel-chested man with steel-grey hair and a kind expression that belied the formal suit he was wearing for the portrait. His hand rested on the woman's shoulder, and two brown Labrador retrievers sat at their feet.

"I think they had it painted here." Beatrice cocked her head and looked down the center aisle of the library. "Under that stained glass window."

"Why do you say that?"

"There's a slightly rosy tint." She pointed at the corner. "See? I bet during the day, that's where the sun hits."

"No, there's a door in that picture, and there's not one on the wall."

"They could have moved it."

"Moved a door in a place like this? With all these stone walls? It's not a matter of moving Sheetrock, tesoro."

"You're probably right." She smiled. "Your friend looks happy. You can see that spark in her eye." Beatrice put her hand in Giovanni's. "We should have a portrait made."

"So there's proof in a hundred years that we're immortal?" He lifted her hand and kissed her knuckles. "It'll end up in a museum and we'll have to have Ben and Tenzin steal it back for us. Better not. Photographs are bad enough."

Beatrice saluted the portrait. "Off we go, Penny. We're going to find your play, and then we'll..." She looked at Giovanni. "What are we going to do with it?"

"We'll decide that when we find it." He pulled Beatrice toward the hall of bookshelves. "Now, my darling fanged bookworm, let's put those vampire senses to good use, shall we? How fast can you sniff out four-hundred-year-old paper?"

Beatrice's eyes lit up. "I do enjoy a challenge."

They spent two hours searching through the first row of bookcases, Beatrice using her keen sense of smell to sniff out any paper older than three hundred years while Giovanni used that time to explore the shelves themselves for hidden compartments, including books that looked out of place or might be hollow.

They hadn't spoken for over an hour, and midnight was approaching when they heard the door of the library creak open.

Beatrice looked for Giovanni, but he was already moving in the shadows to intercept whoever was approaching. In all likelihood it was Nick coming to check on them, but they didn't want to take a chance.

She took a deep breath and froze.

Vampire.

There was a scuffle, then a bitten-out curse in guttural French and a sharp exhalation as Beatrice rounded the corner, the long dagger she kept at her back already drawn.

What she saw was far from what she'd been expecting.

Her husband was standing near the fireplace, a long hunting knife drawn and held at the neck of a golden-haired vampire whose fangs were bared.

Beatrice frowned and lowered her blade. "René?"

B en tossed a piece of popcorn at his sister, expecting a reaction but not the deep and nearly painful eye roll that he received.

"What is that look?" He tried to stifle a laugh but failed.

"You're going to get grease on this shirt, and I have to wear it to school tomorrow." She looked down at the grey shirt with dark black crosses scattered over it. She was wearing that, a black pair of jeans on her awkwardly long legs, and Doc Marten boots she'd probably stolen from her mother's closet.

"You don't have to wear that shirt *exactly*," Ben said. "I have a feeling you have a few others."

"Yeah. I do have to wear this shirt *exactly*."

"Why?"

"Because it's our last day before break and Kaya is going to wear her white shirt with grey crosses and then we'll look badass because we'll look like light and dark twins."

Light and dark twins?

"Let me guess, you're the dark twin?" With her olive-toned skin, nearly black hair, and dark brown eyes, his sister could pull off the baby-goth-princess look with ease. "B must be so proud."

Sadia slouched down in the plush theater seat. "Please, like she even notices."

Oh, so it's like that.

He let a few more minutes of the classic horror movie pass in silence. Beatrice and Giovanni had a vast collection of vintage horror, and Ben had seen them all because Tenzin was perversely fascinated by film depictions of monsters.

Ben tried to be casual. "You know, I remember when your mom was younger. Her style was a lot like yours. Especially when she was wearing her motorcycle leathers."

By the look in her eye, Sadia hadn't heard of the motorcycle-leathers stage in her mother's fashion history.

"Let's just watch the movie." She threw a piece of popcorn back at Ben. "You talk too much."

"Tenzin might have mentioned that once or twice."

Ben kicked his feet up in the movie room that Beatrice had redecorated a few years before. There was a new projector, a larger seating area, and a popcorn machine in the corner.

Growing up with vampires for parents could be more than a little limiting. There were no Saturday movie matinees with friends or trips to the water park in the summer with Mom and Dad. Family life happened at night, and security personnel became part of the family.

After another half hour of watching the movie, he chanced another question. "How's Dema?"

Sadia shrugged. "I don't know. Normal, I guess."

"She seeing Daniel at all?"

"I don't ask her about her love life," Sadia muttered. "Your ovaries are showing, Ben."

He threw his head back and laughed. "I'll remember that one."

The corner of her sullen mouth turned up. "You can use it on Gavin."

"I will."

Beatrice and Giovanni had done what they could to make Sadia's life as normal as possible, sending her to an exclusive school where she was surrounded by the children of vampire employees and a few vampire relatives like her.

Most vampires—if they adopted human children— kept them in seclusion for security reasons. Any vulnerability for a vampire parent was a threat, children more than any other. But naturally, that also produced some pretty messed-up kids that had no idea how to socialize, and Beatrice and Giovanni didn't want that for Sadia.

"So how are your friends at school?"

Without another word, Sadia stood and tossed a handful of popcorn at Ben before she stomped up the stairs of the theater and out the door.

Ben stared after her while a mummy on the screen chased a screaming woman in an evening dress down a creepy hallway dripping with cobwebs.

"What did I say?"

FOUR

"René du Pont." Giovanni carefully pronounced the name. "Son of Guy du Pont, son of Carwyn ap Bryn, one of my oldest and dearest friends."

They were sitting by the fireplace, René in a wingback chair, his legs kicked out in front of him, his jacket laid across the back of the sofa and his sleeves rolled up in casual ease. He looked like a very rich college boy who'd snuck home from the dormitories when mummy and daddy were on holiday.

René rolled his eyes like the adolescent he was. "Son of Guy, blah blah blah. Why stop there? Nephew of Gemma Melcombe. Charming rival of Benjamin Vecchio. Former lover of Tenzin—"

"Bullshit," Beatrice blurted. "She wouldn't give you the time of day."

"No?" The golden-haired immortal smiled. "You'll

have to ask her. Someone told me she had an email file devoted to me. We keep in touch."

Beatrice had no doubt that René continued to be fascinated with Tenzin, but she suspected the feeling wasn't mutual.

Giovanni said, "You're not supposed to be here."

"It's good to see you too." The French vampire smiled with beatific innocence.

"*Why* are you here, René?" Beatrice leaned forward. "You're a thief. What are you trying to steal?"

He narrowed his eyes. "I could ask you the same question. What are *you* trying to steal? I know the human solicitors didn't hire two of the most notorious book thieves in the immortal world to catalog a valuable library."

Giovanni looked down his nose at René as he stood over him. "Book thieves? My mate is a scribe of Penglai. I hardly think that's the reputation she and I have garnered."

"In the vampire world, no, but why don't you ask a collection of human archivists and curators?" He whispered, "You're notorious."

"We're unknown."

René's eyes glowed. "For which I am supremely *jaloux*. Your mastery of stealth is unparalleled, and for that I deeply admire you." He bowed his head slightly. "For me? I cannot even be in this country without risking my dearest uncle's wrath."

"Isn't that because you killed his sire?"

"Not even a little bit!" He looked sincerely perturbed.

"What trouble some of my more notorious friends caused is certainly not my fault, is it? They might have misled me as to their intentions in visiting London."

Beatrice sat on the chaise nearest René's wingback. "Speaking of secret intentions, you haven't answered our question. Why are you here?"

"There could be a journal with some... private information about a certain client of mine. Lord Mortimer absconded with it in some very English expedition over the Khyber Pass just prior to Partition. My client would dearly like his personal property back before human curators come in and start poking into it."

"And I'm assuming your client is...?" Beatrice spread her arms.

"One of us?" René shrugged. "Mais bien sûr. Of course. Who of us has not been annoyed when some over-curious human makes off with our personal papers?"

It was a perfectly valid and reasonable explanation, and Beatrice didn't believe a word of it. "We're looking for something as well," she said. "Lady Penelope was an old friend of Giovanni's, and after she passed, she..."

René's eyes danced. "But of course she left him a personal bequest of some kind. Who am I to question a gift from an old friend? It sounds like we are searching for quite different things, mon amis. Surely the library is big enough for three vampires?"

Giovanni backed away, and Beatrice rose to join him. They walked to the opposite side of the room and lowered their voices, switching to Latin, which René might speak but was far less likely to understand well.

"He could help us look," Beatrice said.

"Do you trust him?"

"Of course not, but what he's looking for actually sounds like a more legitimate claim than ours." Beatrice had to smile. "In this case? We *are* the book thieves."

"Retrieval specialists." Giovanni cast an eye over his shoulder. "He's not dangerous to either of us. He squeaked like a baby bird when I put a knife to his neck."

"His elemental power is earth." She looked around. "He can't manipulate anything here."

"And yet we both agree he's lying?"

"I have zero doubt. About what?" Beatrice lifted a shoulder. "It could be anything. Hell, with René, he could be telling the truth and it only sounds like he's lying, but with him it's impossible to tell the difference."

"Unfortunately, you're right." He glanced at the blond vampire one more time. "Do you think we should tell Ben and Tenzin?"

"And have Ben fly over here just to chop off something René might miss for a few decades?" She shook her head. "Why bother? I say we help him and he helps us. We're looking for different things, and six eyes is better than four."

"We find his journal and we hand it over, and if he finds our play—"

"I do love that you're so proprietary about it already."

"It is ours," he said. "I'm sure Penny would want me to have it. We just haven't found it yet. But if René finds ours, he'll hand it over to us? Will he agree to that?"

"He might." She looked at the dawdling vampire with

his smug expression and foppish appearance. "If he doesn't, it's simple. We call Terry and have him kicked out of England again."

"If Terry catches René in England, we might witness a Shakespearean tragedy right in front of us."

Beatrice turned to René and started walking. "Monsieur du Pont, I think we might have a proposition for you."

Giovanni left Beatrice and René searching the bookshelves in the library while he went to find a kitchen and some tea.

Great old houses tended to resemble a maze, and this one was no different. It was a Jacobean mansion built around a large central courtyard, rising four full stories to a dark slate roof. The formal rooms and family rooms were on the south side with large windows to capture the light. The library, servants' quarters, and working rooms of the house were on the north side.

Giovanni had explored a billiard room, an old-fashioned smoking room, and a truly impressive armory before he managed to catch the scent of vinegar and lemon wax in the air. He followed his nose through the winding halls to the butler's pantry, which in turn led to a large kitchen where a shadowed figure was sitting in the darkness, stirring a spoon in a teacup.

Nick Mortimer looked like a man in grief. There was

sorrow in the angle of his forehead, and when he looked up at Giovanni, there were tears in the corners of his eyes.

He quickly sat up straight and cleared his throat. "Dr. Vecchio, pardon me. The staff has retired for the night, but I'm happy to make you a cup of tea if you are looking for one."

"That would be wonderful." Giovanni realized the meeting was fortuitous. "I am glad we met, Lord—"

"Oh please. Nick is as formal as I like in my home."

"Of course, Nick. I wanted to let you know that because of the library's size, we called in an additional associate to help us catalog. His name is René, and he'll be assisting Beatrice and me during our work."

The young man smiled. "The more the merrier, as Aunt Penny used to say."

"Indeed." Giovanni smiled. "Yes, that was Penny. She loved having a full house for a party."

Nick's smile was bemused. "It's so odd to speak with someone my age who knew Penny. Most of her friends were much older."

Giovanni often forgot that while he was over five hundred years old, he appeared to be no more than a man in his early thirties. "I was fortunate to know Lady Penelope through a dear friend who was her contemporary. He was often a guest at her home in Kent when they were young people. I've enjoyed many of his stories."

Nick stood and walked to the massive range that dominated one wall. "When I was younger, you know, I used to sneak in here for cakes. The cook who worked here when I was young was a soft touch, and she always made extra when the children visited."

"They never had children of their own," Giovanni said. "But they clearly enjoyed your company."

"I think they did want children, but I know Great-Uncle Mort was quite a bit older when they married. And of course he'd been in the war. That may have been a factor." Nick shrugged. "I was closer to Aunt Penny than I was to my grandmothers to be honest. She had a marvelous sense of humor. A passion for the arts. She was always interested in what we had to say even when we were very young."

"An ideal aunt."

"I couldn't imagine one better."

"How old were you when she started telling you rude vicar jokes?"

Nick broke into a smile. "Dear Lord, maybe eleven or twelve? She had a million of them, didn't she? What's worse than the First World War?"

"The vicar's garden party," Giovanni said.

Nick laughed. "Not the most devout woman, was she?"

"I imagine the Almighty is enjoying her vicar jokes in person right now." Giovanni sat at the kitchen table and pictured Penny's bright smile. "She was a light."

"She was. And according to my uncle, the best thing that ever happened to this place. The Mortimers are all a bit crusty as a family, aren't we? Not a very good history all in all. Lots of empire building and political machinations." Nick grimaced. "It will be good to put all that money to good use."

Giovanni perked up. "Do you have a cause of some kind you're supporting?"

"Oh right! I didn't tell you." Nick turned with the kettle and poured boiling water into two large mugs. "Elise and I—Elise Lambert, my fiancée—have a music school planned. Combine my interests and my aunt's."

"That's a wonderful idea. I'm glad your fiancée is supportive. That's very important in a marriage."

"She's a wonderful girl." The man's cheeks turned a little rosy. "I'm a lucky man."

"I'm sure she feels the same."

"Ah… about the school though. I'm hoping that we can focus on areas of the county where music lessons and education might be a luxury that some families can't afford." He dunked tea bags in the mugs. "I think music is a universal right, don't you? It can lift anyone from any situation. Even if they're only listening to music, if they love it, it's…"

"Transporting." Giovanni nodded. "I do know what you mean." He remembered his own childhood. He would often run to church when the choir began to sing. The sound of the mass being sung was the sound of heaven to his childhood ears. "A music school is a wonderful idea, Nick. Your Aunt Penny would be proud."

"Uncle Mort was a fan of the idea too." Nick raised his mug. "He wasn't a musician, but he was a big supporter of education. I believe there's even a school in

Pakistan named after him or something like that. He gave quite a large amount to a community there to modernize their facilities."

"Is that so?" Giovanni kept his face carefully blank. Pakistan.

The Khyber Pass was in northern Pakistan.

Lord Mortimer absconded with it in some very English expedition over the Khyber Pass just prior to Partition.

"Oh yes. He was quite selfless about it too. I don't know that he ever visited, though the head of school sent him updates every term."

"Your uncle," Giovanni began, "did he spend time in Pakistan?"

Nick nodded. "After the war. Some geological expedition, I believe. Something to do with the roads. He was a cartographer as a hobby. So many men of his station had hobbies like that in those years." Nick sipped his tea. "He and my father were quite at odds about it, as a matter of fact. My mother was certain I was wasting my time studying education, but Penny and Mort approved. They said I wouldn't need the money, but I'd turn into a useless fool if I didn't have a focus in life."

"They sound like exceptional people."

Nick smiled. "Uncle Mort could be... well, stern I suppose. But Penny chased those demons away."

There could be a journal with some... private information about a certain client of mine... dearly like his personal property back before human curators come in and start poking into it.

Giovanni found himself wondering exactly who

René's client was, what that expedition in Pakistan had been about, and just what Charles Mortimer had been up to in his youth.

If Penny's husband had demons, where had they come from?

And did they have a name Giovanni could trace back to René du Pont?

FIVE

"We could sell it."

"It has to be performed."

"What if it's shit?"

"It's Shakespeare. You think it's going to be shit?"

"I'm just saying that I slept through *Henry VIII* and I don't think I missed much."

"Only the breakup of the Catholic Church? The birth of one of the greatest monarchs in history?"

"Its performance literally burned down the Globe Theatre—I don't think I'm wrong on this."

"That was not the fault of—"

"Mon Dieu!" René slammed a volume of the *Encyclopaedia Britannica* down on the library table. "Shut up. For fuck's sake, shut up. At this point, I want to burn down this theater myself."

Beatrice looked up from a stack of Marlowe books

that were grouped near the Shakespeare section of the library. "What?"

"I think he regards our Shakespeare debate as tiresome." Giovanni was sitting in a wingback chair, paging through what they'd guessed was an attempt at cataloging by some well-intentioned amateur back in the 1980s. "He's wrong of course."

Beatrice smirked at René. The vampire was smart, that was certain, but patience was not his strong suit. He'd reluctantly agreed to their deal the night before and had even appeared enthusiastic in the early-morning hours when they managed to narrow down the shelves where personal journals seemed to be kept.

The nitty-gritty of cataloging, however, was far from entertaining.

"René, you said there were journals from the 1590s in your section?"

"Yes, but everything appears to be from the Mortimer family collection. If your old friend hid anything of her scandalous ancestress among them, I haven't found it yet."

"Look in the Marlowe," Giovanni muttered. "Penny had a sense of humor."

Beatrice looked up. "Marlowe?"

"Of course." He set down the folded pages he'd been studying and sat up. "Penny loved to tease people. What greater tease than putting an unknown Shakespeare play in a section devoted to his biggest rival?"

Beatrice walked over to the section of the library shelves

she'd identified the night before. She'd spent most of the previous night—after persuading René to join their efforts—mapping the entire library, using vampire speed to create a large grid and identify most of the major sections. Many were jumbled, especially in areas that appeared to be used more. Fiction, poetry, and plays were the most disorganized.

"Marlowe and Shakespeare overlap a little bit here," Beatrice said. "There might be some Marlovians in the Mortimer line."

"It wouldn't matter," Giovanni said. "Look for anything out of place. Penny loved puzzles and games."

Beatrice made short work of looking through the volumes on the shelves. "It's a good collection. All Marlowe's major works except... Hmm." The missing volume was notable. "There's not a single volume of his poetry. Just the plays."

In a second, Giovanni was at her side. "Nothing? Not any of his poetry?"

Beatrice double-checked the shelf. "There are some academic works related to his poetry but not a collected volume in the bunch."

René wandered over too. "A collector would have obtained one at some point, correct?"

Beatrice looked at the other Elizabethan collection. "There are multiple volumes from his contemporaries, and we've already gone through the Mortimer Shake-speare collection. I'm going to say that it's definitely strange the poetry is missing."

"Agreed," Giovanni said. "Especially knowing how

much Penny enjoyed poetry." He nodded. "It's a clue. Not much to go on, but it's something."

"What of these... academic works related to his poems?" René asked. "What of them? Have you looked through those for any leads?"

Beatrice smiled. "Good idea." She pulled a paperbound volume with tabs sticking out. "Here's something from the University of Warwick." She flipped to one of the first tabs. "Uh... an essay here about *Hero and Leander*."

Giovanni perked up. "*Hero and Leander*?"

She looked up. "Based on the Greek story, right?"

"Yes, but it was unfinished." Giovanni held out his hand, and Beatrice gave him the paperbound volume. "If I recall, there were two early editions of the poem published just after Marlowe's death. One was the unfinished one with only Marlowe's verses, and the second contained the conclusion that was written by George Chapman. That's the version that's most familiar now, but any original quarto that dates back to that first printing would be valuable."

René's ears perked up. "How valuable?"

"Depending on the condition, maybe twenty to thirty thousand pounds, but not hundreds of thousands," Giovanni said.

"Mmm." René shrugged. "This is not the play you are looking for. This is not even Shakespeare. We should keep looking."

"It might not be Shakespeare," Beatrice said, "but

Marlowe was an inspiration to Shakespeare. Highly respected."

"He was also a spy." Giovanni frowned.

"Rumored but never confirmed," Beatrice said. "Shakespeare put a shout-out to Marlowe in *As You Like It*, in fact. It was a line from *Hero and Leander*: 'Dead Shepherd, now I find thy saw of might, Who ever lov'd that lov'd not at first sight?'"

"So we're back to Shakespeare by way of Marlowe." Giovanni frowned. "A missing volume of poetry in Marlowe."

Beatrice echoed the thought. "A missing play from Shakespeare?"

He pointed at the Shakespeare collection they'd spread out on the table. "Look through the copies of *As You Like It*, specifically act three."

They all rushed to the table, looking for different volumes. Most of the Shakespeare plays were in thick leather-clad volumes with gilt edging and elaborate binding, but one book stuck out to Beatrice. It was a heavy paperback—clearly well loved by the state of the spine—with a vintage illustration on the cover. It wasn't expensive, and it had numerous notes and papers sticking out.

She opened the front cover to see a university bookstore stamp in the front and a name written on the title page.

Penelope Percy-Reed.

"This is Penny's college copy." She felt the rush of her blood, and her fangs dropped as she paged through to the beginning of the play.

As You Like It.

The letter was notable for the crispness of the paper. This wasn't a mangled note or a receipt or even a well-loved card. Stuck in the middle of the third act was a piece of heavy cream stationery with one name on it.

CASPAR DAVIDSON.

Tenzin sat in the living room, reading one of Giovanni's many journals she'd stolen from his office. It was so silly how the vampire continually changed their location, expecting her not to look for them. What did he expect? That she was just going to accept that he'd had hundreds of years of life and she wasn't entitled to know about it?

Ridiculous.

She heard Sadia walk down the stairs, but she didn't lift her head. In Tenzin's experience, children of Sadia's age responded to benign neglect. One couldn't be too interested in them without garnering disdain, so Tenzin kept her eyes on the curled pages of Giovanni's journal and ignored the girl.

After a few moments, Sadia gave a slight huff and wandered down the hallway toward Caspar and Isadora's wing of the house. Tenzin silently floated from the wing-back by the fireplace to a bench in the hall.

Tenzin eavesdropped mercilessly when it came to the people she cared about, and Sadia was as good as her own child. She'd murder a monk to protect the girl from any real danger, but she was also aware that at age twelve, most of the demons Sadia faced were of her own making.

"Grandma Isa?" Sadia kept her voice soft. "Are you awake?"

Isadora was in her early nineties and slept for much of the day, but she'd lived for many years in a house of vampires, so early evenings were one of her more alert times.

"Sadia." Isadora's voice was strong. "Of course, come in and sit with me. I was going to work on a puzzle. Would you like to help?"

"Sure." The girl seemed to relax around her great-grandmother. "Is it the butterfly puzzle still?"

"Oh no. Your grandfather and I finished that one yesterday. I'm working on the edges of a new landscape."

"Is it a picture from Mexico?"

"How did you know?"

With age came nostalgia. Tenzin remembered Nima's desire to be reminded of her childhood home in her last years. She had surrounded the elderly woman with her favorite food, music from Tibet, and colorful quilts to keep her warm.

"This one is pretty."

"That is a town named Tlaquepaque near Guadalajara. It's not far from where I lived when I was your age."

"Oh, that's nice." There was a long stretch of silence. "I like the umbrellas."

"Aren't they pretty? And the houses there are just as colorful. It's an artists' community."

"You're an artist. Is that why you lived there?"

"Oh no. I wasn't an artist when I was a little girl. I only started taking pictures when I came to this country."

There was more silence as the girl and the old woman worked on the task together.

"Do you think I'll be able to go back to Damascus someday?"

"I'm sure you will, Sadia. Do you want to?"

"Yes." The answer was firm. "But I know it's still dangerous."

"I'm sure it won't always be that way."

"Do you think any of my birth family is alive?"

"If they are, do you know who would be able to find them better than anyone?"

"Mama and Baba."

"That's right."

Tenzin closed Giovanni's journal and set it to the side. Vampires were powerful, immortal, and well-connected, but even they couldn't always overrule human governments. The tragedy of Sadia's family was something she didn't often think about because there was nothing she could do to remedy the loss of the girl's parents.

She knew Giovanni and Beatrice kept Sadia as connected to her Syrian heritage as they could when they lived a covert life among humans. Dema came from a Syrian background. They spoke Arabic with the girl and attended religious services at the Syrian Orthodox Church.

It was a stark contrast to Ben, who had Lebanese

blood but no connection with his mother's family and only limited contact with his father's.

Roots. Blood. Ancestral memory. If she closed her eyes, she felt nothing for them. Her blood had died thousands of years ago. If any of it survived, it was a diffuse diaspora across Central Asia.

But Sadia wasn't five thousand years old—she was twelve.

The girl sighed. "Do you think they'll be back before Christmas?"

"I suspect they will. Caspar is on a video call with your father right now. Do you want to talk to him? I'm sure they'd love to see you."

"No. Mom texted me this morning. It's cool."

The girl sounded thoughtful but not saddened by her parents' absence. Good. Sadia was cosseted and protected far more than she would like. Any hint of independence was likely welcome.

"You've found a lot of pieces on the bottom border," Isadora said. "Nicely done."

"No problem," Sadia said. "I like doing puzzles with you. I mean... they're not little-kid puzzles, so it's cool."

"Well, you're not a child, so I wouldn't expect you to enjoy children's puzzles."

Sadia let out a huge sigh. "I wish everyone else thought that way."

"What way? That you're not a child?"

"Yes." The exasperation was clear, even from a distance. "It's like, Ben comes and expects me to want to watch cartoons with him. Tenzin basically ignores me, and Dema is hovering. I swear, she's just hovering over my every move. It's embarrassing."

"Well, she is your bodyguard, and your parents are out of the country, so I expect that's related to work."

"Fine. I mean... yeah, that's okay I guess." The girl began to get choked up. "I just wish everyone knew..."

"Oh sweetheart." Isadora was clearly concerned. "What is it, my love?"

"I don't know!"

The girl was obviously crying. Tenzin could hear the sniffles and practically saw the tears welling in her eyes. Her scent had changed from her distress and...

Her scent.

"Oh, my sweet girl." Isadora was in full comforting-grandmother mode. "Is there anything I can do? Should I talk to—?"

"No! Don't talk to anyone! There's nothing wrong. I'm just... tired I guess. Or something."

"Okay." Isadora reassured her. "It's all going to be all right. I'm here for *you*, Sadia. You can tell me anything that's bothering you. I will always protect your confidence. Do you believe me?"

"Yeah." The girl sniffed. "I know. I love you, Grandma."

"I love you too. So very much."

"Do you have any chocolate?"

"Of course." Isadora's voice took on a note of clarity. "Every woman—no matter her age—should have a treat for herself hidden away for times like this."

Ah, it made sense now. It all made sense.

Hormonal changes were easily detectable by experienced vampires. Ben hadn't been around long enough to sense the rush of hormones that was flooding his younger sister's system, but that wasn't the case for Tenzin.

Sadia might not know why she was so moody and upset for absolutely no reason.

But Tenzin did.

Six

"My goodness." Caspar's face was soft and thoughtful. "I wonder when she wrote that."

"I hope you forgive me reading it to you," Giovanni was sitting in their rooms at Graves Court, speaking to Caspar on the screen while Beatrice readied herself for the evening. "We think it might be a clue."

"No, I understand completely." He smiled a little. "Such a Penny thing to do, isn't it? Make a little game of it, all for her own amusement. She loved doing things like that. Do you remember, Giovanni?"

"I do. She was the queen of treasure hunts during house parties."

"I love the idea that she's looking down, amused that you're still alive and reading my letters."

Giovanni held up the letter. "Clever of you to tell her I am my own grandson."

"Two generations makes the resemblance a little less

alarming." He chuckled. "That and failing vision helped the ruse." He shifted in his seat. "Read the last bit again."

"Not the first paragraph about her fond memories of—"

"No, that's quite enough of that." Caspar cleared his throat.

"Are you blushing, old man?"

"At least that means my blood's still flowing, you fossil."

"So little respect..." Giovanni picked up the letter and skimmed down to the last part. "'You'll remember my dear old aunt Rosalind and her antics in the forest. She was always stealing Orlando's poems and hiding them in the wrong trees. So silly of her that Love's wit became her Face in Ben's best story.'"

"The last part makes absolutely no sense," Caspar said. "Rosalind? I'm assuming she's referring to her aunt who dressed like a young man in order to act on the stage—"

"A clear reference to Rosalind in *As You Like It*," Giovanni said. "The second part of it though..."

"Stealing Orlando's poems?"

"The play perhaps? Orlando was Rosalind's lover. Is she implying that her ancestor and Shakespeare were lovers?"

"It would explain why he gave her the play."

Giovanni looked up from the letter. "I wonder if there are reports of which actors played Rosalind at the Globe. Wouldn't it be fantastic if the actor playing

Rosalind was a woman dressing as a man, playing a woman pretending to be a man?"

"My God, what a tangled web." Caspar burst into laughter. "She's laughing at the both of us, Gio."

"I know she is." Giovanni shook his head. "Incorrigible Penny." He tapped the letter. "What do you think of this bit though? '...stealing Orlando's poems and hiding them in the wrong trees.' Trees could imply wood. Wood makes bookshelves?"

"So she's hidden Orlando's poems in the wrong bookshelves?" Caspar nodded. "It works. But the last part..."

"It's obviously code for something, but I can't relate it to anything in Shakespeare." Giovanni stared at the note. "Love's wit. Love... face? Is that a name? I can't remember." He turned when he heard Beatrice coming through the door. "Love's wit, dearest wife. Does it bring anything to mind from Shakespeare's work?"

Beatrice was strapping on a pair of daggers under her jacket. "Love's wit?" She frowned. "I don't... Shakespeare? Are we sure it's Shakespeare?"

He spotted the daggers. "Why the blades?"

"Protection." Beatrice was a water vampire of considerable power, but she did enjoy a good sword, particularly when abundant water sources weren't around. "Don't forget who our accomplice is."

"*Accomplice* makes it sound so..."

"Illegal?" She grinned. "Hello, Caspar."

"Who is your accomplice this time?"

"Gemma's nephew," Giovanni said. "The French one that belongs to Guy."

Caspar leaned toward the screen. "Are you speaking of René du Pont? Didn't he try to kill Benjamin on multiple occasions?"

Giovanni lifted both his hands slowly. "I feel that one is open for debate. According to Tenzin—"

"Wait." Beatrice stopped him. "When did René try to kill Ben?"

The switch from relaxed thief to dangerous mother was swift.

"As I said, according to Tenzin, it was all in good fun. He saved their life in Romania. I think."

Beatrice narrowed her eyes. "You get your information from Tenzin, and she tells you" —Beatrice pinched her fingers together— "approximately ten percent of the truth and forty percent what she'd like the truth to be."

He rocked in the swivel chair by the desk. "And what happened to the other fifty percent of all that?"

"She doesn't tell you that part at all." She looked at the letter in Giovanni's hand. "It's not Shakespeare. We have to look broader. Remember, the first clue was in Marlowe's section. Missing poetry. Missing play."

"Is this reference to Marlowe?" Giovanni held up the letter. "I'm fairly well-versed in his work, and I don't—"

"Not Marlowe." She plucked the letter from his hand. "Love's wit in Ben's best story." She looked at Caspar. "Ben, not Will or Kit. Ben Jonson. Ben's best story is *The Alchemist*. Love's wit is Lovewit, one of the main characters. And Face...?" She cocked her head. "It's another character. The butler, I think?"

Giovanni turned to Caspar. "The butler?"

"Well, now I'm embarrassed that I didn't guess it," Caspar said. "So obviously your next task is to find a copy of *The Alchemist*." He waved at the screen. "I have a feeling that Penny's next clue will be there."

Beatrice patted her sides as she approached the library doors, reassuring herself that her daggers were there and within easy reach. Nick had opened the front door on her first knock, much to the dismay of the irritated housekeeper, and shown her into the library where René du Pont was already at work.

Not in the Renaissance literature area. No, the French vampire was rustling about in the maps and geology section.

Beatrice crept toward him in utter silence and slowly let her amnis spread outward, flooding the air with her energy until René dropped the book in his hand and spun toward her.

"Beatrice."

She leaned against a heavy bookcase. "René."

The vampire dragged his gaze up and down her body. "May I say you look stunning in leather?"

"You may, because it's the truth." She'd dressed for comfort that night, in jeans and a simple black T-shirt, her leather jacket concealing her weapons. "What are you doing?"

He shrugged. "You have your job; I have mine. I am looking for the journal, of course."

"In the geology section?"

"Charles Mortimer was an amateur geologist, no? That was why he was with the British Army in the Khyber Pass. My thought was that the journal he absconded with might be contained in some records from his trip there."

It was actually a decent theory, so she let it pass. "Did you try to kill my nephew?"

He barely blinked. "I believe that could be classified as a misunderstanding."

"Twice?"

René frowned. "Twice seems excessive. I really only meant him harm once." He frowned. "And to be fair, he has tried to kill me an equal number of times."

"Was he human or vampire?"

René smirked. "That one has always been vampire. Even when he was human, he was vampire."

"Fair point," she muttered. "Come on. We're looking for a Ben Jonson play tonight."

René looked over her shoulder. "And where is your charming mate? Wiping the memory of the human and his fiancée?"

That brought Beatrice up short. "Is the girlfriend back? Did you meet her?"

"No, the housekeeper mentioned her, but we did not

meet." René started toward the Renaissance fiction section. "And Giovanni?"

"One of Terry's men took him to London." She followed René down the center aisle. "He had some questions for a dealer there that he knows. Probably trying to feel out what this play could potentially be worth."

"Millions, obviously. A genuine first folio recently sold for just under ten million US."

She smiled. "Doing your research, I see."

"Mon Béatrice, this library is a gold mine." He turned, spreading his arms out and looking around the massive bookcases. "Do you know how many valuable editions are in here? And completely unguarded. I could break into this place with my... pinky finger." He held it up. "Perhaps I have been sleeping on the rare book market."

"One thing to know about the rare book world is that it's all about reputation," Beatrice said. "Which is an area you might have trouble with."

"Perhaps." René narrowed his eyes. "And Giovanni?"

"Always works through intermediaries," she said. "Like this associate in London. The play will have to be authenticated. Provenance documented. It's not a matter of showing up with an old pile of paper and expecting it to be taken seriously. Even if we find it, there will be scholars who will make their careers on proving or disproving its authenticity."

René's smile grew. "So much controversy. Delicious."

"Delicious maybe, but it can be costly too." She pushed past him. "Let's get to work. The play we're looking for is called *The Alchemist*. It'll probably be grouped with other plays. Look for something like *The Works of Ben Jonson*. It'll probably be a volume like that. Any age is possible."

"And when will Giovanni return?"

She reached a section that appeared to contain miscellaneous Renaissance playwrights and started to take out volumes and set them on the table. "Tomorrow night maybe. Probably the next night. It's a few hours' drive to London, and this man might not be able to meet tonight; he's eighty-five."

"Your husband does like to mingle with the elderly, doesn't he?" René dragged a rolling ladder over and climbed up the bookcase.

"Giovanni may look like a Roman god in his prime, but he's over five hundred years old." She found another bound edition and pulled it. "From his perspective, eighty-five is hanging out with the youths."

I t was another stormy night in Los Angeles, and by stormy, Ben absolutely was thinking of his twelve-year-old sister and her moods.

Sadia huffed out of the room, clutching her phone and furiously texting with... someone.

"Who?" He turned to Zain, the house manager and cook, who was clearing dishes from dinner. "Who does she text? Why is she angry? What did I do?"

Zain tried to hide his smile, but it was unmistakable. "Probably Kaya, her best bestie who's the only other kid in her class who has vampire parents."

"Oh. Well, that's good. When I was in school, I was the only one who— Never mind that. What is she so pissed off about? What did I do?"

"I believe you asked her to clear her plate."

"The horror." Ben blinked. "Was that unreasonable somehow?"

"She was already going to do that." Zain looked at the three empty water glasses on the end of the counter. "Obviously."

"Oh my God." Ben was starting to get exasperated. He didn't think he was old. Was he old? He knew he didn't look a day over twenty-nine, but maybe he was old? "Wait, am I old?"

"To her?" Zain nodded. "We're all old. We're all out of touch. None of us understand her, and we're all unreasonable."

"I'm her big brother, not her dad."

Zain shook his head. "Doesn't matter."

Ben rubbed his hands through his hair, yanking at the roots. "I don't know how Gio and B handle this. Every night?"

"Every night. Every day." Zain dropped his voice. "Things are... volatile. That's all I'll say."

Tenzin floated into the room carrying Isadora in her arms. "She wanted to."

Isadora's face was lit up like a Christmas light. "No wonder Sadia loved flying so much when she was young."

Ben couldn't help but picture Isadora flipping in the air and the sound of a cracked hip. "Tiny—"

"It's fine." Tenzin gently placed Isadora at the end of the table on the cushion that was placed there especially for her. "She's fine, Ben. Sadia is right; you *are* old."

He kicked out and knocked the back of her knee. "Take it back."

She winked at him. "You can prove her wrong later when we're alone. I know why Sadia is emotionally unstable."

Zain walked over to bring Isadora a small plate. "Because she's twelve?"

Ben rolled his eyes and took a drink of water. "Sounds about right."

"No, because she's ready to menstruate."

The water spurted out of his mouth and across the kitchen table, hitting Zain in the chest.

"Dude." The man looked down. "Not cool."

"I'd say within the week, judging by her hormone levels."

"Tenzin, what the hell?" Ben did the math. Twelve was probably right. Oh God, was this happening on his watch? Was he going to have to talk to— No. *Don't be ridiculous, Ben.* She'd probably already talked to B. She had to know the mechanics of... all that. "Why would you even say that?"

"Because it's a biological reality?" Tenzin looked confused. "Biology will take care of itself, but we will need to prepare."

"I suspect she already has... supplies for that kind of thing." Ben looked at Zain. "Right?"

The other man shrugged. "You're asking me?"

Dema. Dema would know.

Tenzin shook her head. "I'm not talking about menstruation supplies. Surely there are initiation rites she will need to perform. A ceremony of some kind?" Tenzin looked at Isadora. "What did you do when you started menses as a young woman to celebrate your burgeoning fertility?"

Zain dropped a pan in the sink. "And I'm out. I'll finish this in the morning."

"Oh my God." Ben took a deep breath. "Tenzin, please don't say *burgeoning fertility*."

Zain was already headed toward the door. "Isa, you need anything before I retire for the night?"

"Tenzin was going to make me some tea."

"Why?" Ben whispered to himself. "I could have fallen in love with Chloe, right? I was in love with Chloe once."

Isadora said, "When you were sixteen."

"That's a good idea." Tenzin rapped her fingers on the table and rubbed Ben's back. "We should call Chloe. She's a contemporary woman and would have a better idea of the current cultural practices about fertility rites."

Ben's head shot up. "There will be no fertility rites!"

"What's wrong with fertility?" Tenzin asked. "It's creative power. Women have been honored through history for their goddess-like power of carrying life in the womb."

Isadora said, "I believe he's uncomfortable with the idea that his little sister is... fertile."

He put his head on the table again. "You just keep saying it."

"No one is suggesting she start having *babies*, Benjamin, but it's an important moment in her life."

"Agreed," Isadora said. "And Benjamin, I'm disappointed in you. Half the population menstruates. There shouldn't be any taboo about it."

"I'm not saying it's taboo." He lifted his head. "If she has questions" —he died a little inside, but he pressed on — "I will answer them. I will go and buy her maxipads or tampons or... whatever she needs."

"We used moss and rags when I was human," Tenzin said. "Modern sanitary practices are such an improvement."

"But we" —he motioned between him and Tenzin— "are not the people to be talking about fertility rites with my sister. I don't think they do special ceremonies or anything, Tenzin. She'd probably be embarrassed."

His mate was horrified. "What? There are no ceremonies?" She looked at Isadora. "Do girls not tell the men now? Are they secret rites?"

Isadora smiled a little. "We didn't talk about any of that when I was a girl, even with our mothers or sisters. I was raised in a very strict Catholic home, and I learned from my nanny and the housekeeper."

"You didn't even *speak* about it?" Tenzin looked at both of them with wide eyes. "I was celebrated with a roasted goat and a bonfire. My mother put flowers in my hair, and the women in the village danced. That's when I received my first tattoo."

Isadora's eyebrows went up. "I didn't know you had tattoos. Can vampires get tattoos?"

"Only before they turn." She spun toward Ben. "We are not allowing this moment to pass with no celebration! What is wrong with your culture?"

A moment later, she flew off down the hall.

Probably looking for Sadia so she can tattoo her.

"Tenzin."

"She's gone." Isadora folded her hands on the table. "You can make me my tea."

"Good." Ben rose. "Tea I can handle."

"Periods you can't?"

"Fertility rites," he muttered under his breath as he started the kettle on the stove. "Well, good to know that both of them hate me now."

SEVEN

The following night, Beatrice sat with Nick in the drawing room, trying to pry information out of him, though she was beginning to think the man was clueless about his family's assets and archives. The housekeeper, Mrs. Dawson, was serving them wine and cheese while Nick stared into the fire.

"You seem concerned." Beatrice didn't like to see that many lines on such a young face. "I hope we're not being an imposition. I'm sure it's strange to have so many people in your house, rummaging around in the middle of the night, especially right after your aunt has passed."

"No, no." He stopped himself. "Well, it is odd, but I'm sure you have your reasons. Is your husband—?"

"In London at the moment." She pulled a card from her pocket. "Consulting with E. M. Macintosh on an early Marlowe folio we found." It was the cover story Giovanni had concocted before he left. "Gio wanted to get his opinion before we attempted to put any kind of value on it. It's an early volume and probably quite valuable."

"Oh." His eyebrows went up. "You know, I don't think there's any kind of security or anything on the library. Do you think I should install something? I always assumed most of what's in there were old textbooks and maps and things to do with the estate."

"Once we're finished with our initial survey, we'll know more." Security would definitely be a good thing, but she didn't want to put Nick's alarms up when he was so trusting.

At least not until they were done.

She smiled. "René said that your fiancée returned from her trip."

Nick let out a breath and smiled. "She has. Elise had a wonderful time in town, but I'm happy to have her home. Well, in what will be our home eventually, won't it? She's packing up some things in the cottage tonight. Thought she'd start bringing some of them over in the morning. She has a couple of friends with a van, and she asked them over from town to help."

"A big transition for both of you." Beatrice eyed the housekeeper's back as she left the room. "How does Elise feel about marrying into the aristocracy?" Beatrice caught herself. "I'm sorry—she may already be upper class. I have no idea—"

"Oh no, it's a conversation." Nick laughed. "She was born in France as a matter of fact. Thinks all the titled stuff is rather... Well, it's a different culture, isn't it? She's not sure about being a lady of the manor, but she says she loves me enough to manage it."

"Did she and your aunt get along?"

"Like fast friends," Nick said. "I think Penny is the only reason Elise is willing to move. That and my plan for the music school."

"The music school?"

"Yes, I was telling your husband I'd like to make music education in the country my project, but more locally, I'd like to turn the cottage where Elise and I have been living into a school. It's close enough to town that children would be able to ride their bikes or walk out there, and it's isolated enough that drums and trumpets wouldn't bother anyone."

"That's a great idea," Beatrice said. "Do you think—?"

"Nick?" A young woman poked her head in the door. "Oh. So sorry, I didn't realize you had company."

Nick rose as soon as he saw her. "Elise darling, this is Beatrice De Novo, one of the specialists cataloging the library for the solicitors. We were just talking about the school." He turned to Beatrice with a huge smile. "This is my fiancée, Elise Lambert."

"How lovely." The woman was probably in her early thirties, around Nick's age, and her accent was slight but delicately French. She had rich brown hair and pale skin with a slight flush from the cold outside. "I came to see if you've eaten anything. Did Mrs. Dawson make you eat?"

"I've forgotten again." He smiled and looked at Beatrice. "She knows how forgetful I am."

The young woman reached out her hand. "Look, you must eat." She glanced at Beatrice. "He's terrible about this. Come, Nicholas. I'll warm something in the kitchen." She looked at Beatrice again and her eyes held. "Nothing for you to eat in here, is there?"

It was quick but telling. There was a look, a knowing, a moment of awareness in Elise's eyes.

"Nothing but a bit of cheese," Beatrice said. "Go ahead, Nick. I'm really not thirsty, and I have a lot of work to do."

The woman gave Beatrice a slight nod, then drew Nick into the hallway, away from the fire, the wine, and the strange woman.

Beatrice had no way of knowing how Elise had discerned it, but there was no question in her mind that the woman knew Beatrice was a vampire.

René was paging carefully through a large leather-bound volume on the library table when Beatrice returned. "I have found what I think are all the Ben Jonson volumes in this section and have put them on the table. I put everything else back in slightly better order than we found it." He spread his arm. "So I suggest that we focus on this group."

"Nick's fiancée knows I'm a vampire."

That got René's attention. "How?"

"That's a question, isn't it?" Beatrice walked through

the library, checking the windows and the one door at the back of the room, which led to a mudroom attached to the back of the house. "There was just a look in her eyes, and I know that look."

"Yes, we all know that look," he muttered. "Some of them, they know. They sense our strangeness, I think. The others? Pfft." He waved a hand. "They know nothing."

"Nick is oblivious," she said. "He doesn't even seem to think it's strange we only work at night." Beatrice's senses were raring. She could hear every sweep of paper in the room, every scuttle of a rodent along the wall. The moths near the green library lamp fluttered in a delicate cacophony, and the air smelled of dust, candle wax, and mold.

"Do you think she will tell him?"

"Tell him what?" Beatrice wasn't as worried about that as she was about the sudden, ominous weight of knowledge in the manor. "She probably knows he'd never believe her."

"You and your professor vampire..." René sighed. "I was going to break in and forage in the darkness, wiping the minds of anyone who caught me," he said. "You are Giovanni are so... polite."

Beatrice tried to focus on the job at hand. She opened a volume and looked for the table of contents to search for *The Alchemist*.

The Alchemist. To find a clue from Penny. To find a play that might or might not exist.

"Allegedly," she whispered.

"Allegedly what?"

"Nothing." She didn't want to let on to René that she wasn't certain that this lost Shakespeare play was anything more than a game that Lady Penny was playing with an old flame. "Any luck?"

"I am always lucky." René lifted his chin and looked down his nose at the dusty book he was paging through. "I make certain of it."

They worked in silence for another three hours, but they had no luck, contrary to René's assertion. They still had two more large volumes of collected poetry to go when Beatrice heard something in the mudroom.

Her eyes narrowed on the door. "René?"

"Yes?" He looked up. "Someone is here."

"Yes." She quietly set down the book and walked soundlessly toward the door, padding toward the noise she heard coming from the far room. René moved behind her, as silent as she was.

She stopped her breathing and winced when the door squeaked on its hinges.

René let out a slight humph when they saw what was making the noise. "It is a dog."

Sitting in the middle of the cramped mudroom was a scruffy hound of some sort, long legged and damp up to its knees.

"I thought all the dogs lived in the stables."

René walked past Beatrice and crouched down, holding his hand out for the animal to sniff. "This one must have found its way into the house. Hallo, toutou." He scratched the animal behind the ears. "Look at you, my beautiful girl. What are you doing in this big house on your own?"

Another creak had Beatrice looking beyond the mudroom to the hallway where a door was cracked open and she could see a drift of snow coming under the door.

"René?"

He was busy making friends with the dog. "Yes?"

"I don't think we're alone in the house."

The Frenchman fell immediately still, turned his head toward the door, and rose silently, his fangs already down.

"The back door." He kept his voice barely audible. "Villains?"

"I don't know."

They tiptoed past the gun safe and through the room, which was scattered with boots and gardening equipment, hunting gear, walking sticks, and stacks of old clay pigeons they nearly tripped over. René nearly fell when his shoelace caught on a ski poking out from a rack on the wall.

"Why don't they have a bigger mudroom in a house this large?" René complained.

"And take away from the library?" Beatrice managed to make it through the maze and opened the hallway door, which thankfully swung on silent hinges.

The back door to the open courtyard—the one that led to the servants' hallway where the kitchen, the pantry, the mudroom, and the butler's pantry branched off—was open a crack, no doubt the circumstance that had allowed the friendly hound entry to the main house.

Beatrice took off her jacket, hung it on a hook by the

door, and unsheathed a slightly curved dagger. As she turned, she saw that René already had his own blade drawn.

"Security?" Beatrice whispered.

"One can never be too careful about personal safety." He nodded at the kitchen.

Beatrice heard footsteps behind the door.

René said, "That room first."

"The housekeeper?"

René shook his head. "Smells like a man."

She took a deep breath. "Smells like—"

The door swung open and Nick appeared, a mug of tea in his hand and his eyes wide at the sight of two book authentication experts holding foot-long blades.

Nick blinked. "Oh dear."

"Someone is in the house." Beatrice willed her fangs to retract.

"Well, of course they are." Nick frowned. "Why do you have knives out? Elise and I are staying here tonight, and Mrs. Dawson and Barnes and the stable master—you haven't met him, but his name is—"

"My lord, I do believe these people are not of your household." René bent and picked up a broken lockpick by the open back door. "You have... intruders."

"Oh dear." He looked at Beatrice. "I suppose I should have been more serious about getting a security system in place."

René was staring at the lockpick, his eyes narrowed on the slim piece of metal.

And just like with Elise, she knew.

Beatrice grabbed Nick by the arm and captured René's right ear in a vicious pinch.

"Ow! Mon Dieu, what are you doing?" René hissed.

Nick whispered, "Shouldn't we—?"

"Later."

Nick was starting to realize the gravity of the situation because his voice rose slightly. "Oh dear."

Beatrice dragged the man and the vampire into the mudroom, releasing Nick and shutting the heavy oak door as quietly as possible before she turned on her "accomplice."

"Okay, René." She kept her voice low. "Time to give me your knife and tell me what you're *really* doing in this library."

EIGHT

"The former Lord Mortimer was an amateur geologist," René said. "The kind the British government loved to use for secret expeditions because they didn't have to pay them and they could rarely be bribed."

"Debatable," Nick muttered. "But in the case of my great-uncle, probably correct."

René held Beatrice's gaze. "We spoke of an expedition earlier this week. A notable one that led through the Khyber Pass before the Partition of Pakistan. Mortimer was on that trip and happened to be with a small company when they stumbled upon something unexpected."

Knowing René's true line of work, Beatrice made the logical leap. "Treasure of some kind?"

"A cache of valuables that belonged... *had* belonged to some ancient prince." He cast Beatrice a loaded look. "The others in the company spoke of gold and idols, ceremonial weapons, and jewels of countless color and enormous value."

Certainly not an unusual cache for a vampire, and certainly something he or she would be very annoyed to lose, particularly if that vampire really *was* an ancient prince.

Princes of any age tended to be entitled, whether they were immortal vampires or humans.

"Oh my," Nick said. "Uncle Charles never talked about that. He was very vague about his time in Asia."

Beatrice turned to Nick. "Didn't you say your uncle funded various schools in Pakistan?"

"Yes." Nick's eyes went wide. "You think it was guilt money. These men stole these treasures."

"It's certainly the most likely explanation," René said, "because when my client hired me to find Mortimer's journal—"

"Wait, what journal?" Nick frowned. "I thought you worked for Beatrice and—"

"Nick." Beatrice cut him off. "For now, please hold your questions so I can determine who has broken into your house and how dangerous they are." She heard a creak on the stairs. Not wind vampires, but they could be vampires of other elements. "René, did they hire anyone besides you?"

"It's entirely possible. I was sent to look for information. Others may have been sent to look for the treasure itself."

"You think the treasure from Pakistan is in the house?" Nick leaned in.

Beatrice shot him a look.

"Sorry." He looked up. "Wait, so you think treasure *hunters* are in this house? Right now? Because they think Uncle Charles and Aunt Penny had some sort of treasure hidden here?" His eyes turned from curious to panicked. "Elise! Mrs. Dawson. Dear God, we need to call the p—"

Beatrice reached up, put a hand on the man's neck, and sent him to sleep.

"I can't deal with his questions right now," she said. "You take Nick and find someplace to hide. I'll find whoever is in the house and take care of them."

"You need my help," René hissed. "There is only one of you, and we both heard multiple footsteps. There are at least two other—"

"You think I trust you?" Beatrice hissed. "If I see you behind me, René du Pont, I'm going to assume you're in league with whoever dropped those lockpicks. Lockpicks that you recognized. I will not be understanding, and I will *not* wait for an explanation."

His face went blank.

"I know you know who's here. At least one of them."

"It doesn't make sense," he said. "She's not the type to—"

"Human or vampire?"

He sighed. "Human. But she works for vampires."

"Who?"

"Whoever pays her the most. She's good at what she does."

"And what is that?"

"Cons. Theft. She's an excellent lockpick and an even better actress."

Beatrice had heard enough. Vampires in this house, looking for a mountain of treasure, possibly in the service of the vampire whom Mortimer and the British Army had stolen from in the first place.

It was far from a safe little book hunt in the English countryside.

She snapped her fingers, pointed René to the library door, and unsheathed her second dagger.

René hoisted the tall English gentleman over his shoulder and walked to the library door, opening it as the dog trotted behind. "Me traiter comme un enfant..."

That left Beatrice alone in the mudroom of Audley Manor with two knives, no backup, and an unknown number of vampires and humans infiltrating the house.

Gio, you picked a hell of a time to visit your old book friend.

She crept out of the mudroom on silent feet and headed for the stairs.

"The Mortimer Library, eh?" Edward Macintosh leaned forward and took his glass of neat whiskey with a trembling hand. "That's a great old place. Black hole to most collectors though. Those old families hoard their treasures like they're gold. Well, until they need money. But the Mortimers are rolling in wealth."

Giovanni sat next to the fire, gently coaxing it so the old man wouldn't need to bend down and add wood. "Caspar and I were sad to hear about Penny's passing."

"God, what a character she was." Edward smiled. "Pure delight. Old Morty never deserved her, but he did adore her. I'll give him that."

Giovanni kicked his feet toward the fire and settled in for a gossip about old times. "Do you think she married him for the money?"

Edward sighed. "Possibly. The Percy-Reeds were quite in need of a cash influx around that time if I remember correctly, and Penny was the sacrificial lamb. But I think they were happy. We ran in the same circles until the late 1980s or so. Then she moved out to the country permanently to be closer to the family and we lost touch. She still wrote occasionally though. She'd send me things she found in the library when she wanted my opinion or she needed repairs."

"She didn't have a bad life from what I could tell. Her great-nephew seems like a very nice young man." Giovanni swirled the gold whiskey in the glass. He'd have to head back to Hereford soon if he was going to make it before dawn, but it was lovely to catch up with an old friend.

Edward Macintosh was the son of a printer and one of Giovanni's oldest intermediaries. There wasn't a collector in London who knew more about Elizabethan folios and the market.

"You know if and when we find it, I'll bring it to you first."

Edward's bushy grey eyebrows went up. "You want to sell?"

Giovanni shrugged. "I'll have to talk to Beatrice. The money isn't the issue. We may end up donating it in the end. The important thing is the discovery. A play wants to be performed, doesn't it?"

"Agreed." Edward's eyes twinkled behind the thick lenses of his glasses. "Can you imagine the ruckus? The experts in Oxford will be debating when I'm worm food."

"I'll endeavor to present it to the public in time for you to enjoy at least some of the hubbub." He smiled. "That is if we can find it."

"I've no doubt you will. You seem to find anything you put your mind to."

Giovanni reached out a hand and swirled the fire to drive away the chill in Edward's old shop. "Where did the Mortimers get their money?"

"Oh, the typical wealth of the oldest families." The old man held his wrinkled hands toward the fire. "Land. I believe their house goes back to the Normans. They have farms and tenants. They had coal once upon a time, and mills. Some interests in India if I remember correctly."

"Hmm. The whole library is interesting, but the play comes from Penny's collection, not her husband's family."

"Ah, so it's not really *stealing*." Edward winked. "You're just retrieving it from the Mortimer vault."

Giovanni smiled. "I wouldn't call the library a vault, but yes, you get the idea."

Edward frowned. "I believe they do have a vault

though. I remember a colleague, who shall remain anonymous, mentioning it because he'd consulted on the construction."

Giovanni's interest piqued again. "A vault in the library?"

"Something like that. Charles Mortimer was quite specific about the ventilation because he didn't want the books to spoil. Good of him to think of it, honestly, because you can't imagine the kind of damage I've seen to beautiful manuscripts that sat in a dank old castle for too long. It's an absolute crime the kind of damage dampness can do to—"

"Did Penny know about the vault?" A vault? An actual vault? How had they missed that? There was nothing in the library that even hinted at a vault or a locked section. Could it be in another part of the house they hadn't explored? Was that where Penny had hidden the play?

Edward blinked. "I have no idea if Penny knew. I would assume she did, but I can't remember if she mentioned it in her letters." He rose and reached for his cane. "Did I tell you that you've solved a problem for me, Gio?" The old man walked slowly over to a table near the old desk he used as a sales counter. "I'm going to send this back with you instead of calling the family. Much more direct. Penny sent a book in about six months ago to get the binding redone, and I've been dawdling on it."

"Oh?"

"She told me to bring it with me and come for a visit when I was done. That she missed her old friends." He shuffled some papers and files away from a package wrapped in brown paper. "I was trying to find someone to take me out to Hereford for a visit, but then I saw the announcement in the newspaper." He stopped and sighed. "Don't wait to visit the people you like, Giovanni Vecchio. Our generation is passing."

Giovanni saw the echoes of Caspar's gait in Edward's shuffling feet. "I'm glad we had time to visit, my friend."

"As am I."

The man tried to lift the package, but Giovanni saw his hands tremble and he shot out of his seat.

"Let me."

"You're a good vampire," the old man said. "Kind to old people, and if you ever drank my blood, you wiped any memory of it from my mind." He left the wrapped package on the desk. "Penny said it was a favorite and not particularly valuable historically, so she wanted a fresh binding. I tried to do the old book justice."

Giovanni saw the loose edge of the wrapping paper and slid a finger toward the seam. "May I?"

"I'm sure she would have been delighted for you to appreciate it," Edward said. "The young man who finished the lettering is an artist."

Giovanni slid the tape away from the paper and drew the wrapping back, somehow already knowing the title he'd see beneath his hand.

"She had all sorts of notes and bookmarks in the thing—even a few pressed flowers." Edward was amused. "I kept everything intact. I'm sure every bit and bob had meaning for her."

"I'm sure it did."

The gilt lettering on the front of the volume was surrounded by a filigree of Victorian-style scrollwork that bled into a star-and-planet pattern highlighting the words on the cover.

The Alchemist. 1612. A DRAMATIC PLAY BY BEN JONSON.

"I am absolutely not discussing this anymore." Ben stomped into the guesthouse where he and Tenzin were sheltering during the day. "It's none of our business, Tenzin!"

She was flabbergasted that he had so little respect for this important rite of passage. "This is why your culture is so damaged," she said. "You have no rituals. You have no rites. Your biggest holiday centers around buying things you don't need."

"Gift giving is not about the cost or the act of buying." He was falling back into an old argument. "The cost of the gift isn't the point—it's the thought behind it. You could get me a rock—"

"I thought you wanted a ring."

Ben blinked. "Do not try to distract me. We're talking about my sister."

"Fine. You say that the gift isn't about the cost but the meaning behind it."

He frowned but nodded. "Yes, but—"

"It's not the ritual itself that is important," Tenzin said. "It's the thought behind it, the connection to her past and her ancestors, the connection to the divine feminine and her connection to the earth."

He opened his mouth, then closed it. Then opened it.

You look like a fish.

She didn't say it; he would have been offended. It was the first thing that her assistant and friend Chloe had emphasized about being in an intimate relationship with a man that she actually cared about. They were very sensitive. You couldn't just compare their mouths to fishes. Or their penis to specific species of wild mushrooms, because they would be offended.

She'd had to learn by experience on the second one.

So Tenzin didn't tell Ben that he looked like a fish when he was searching for something to say, but he did resemble one.

Once you say it, you can't unsay it.

It was obvious advice but wise nonetheless.

Ben finally found the words he wanted to say. "Tenzin, I think Sadia would be embarrassed if we made a big deal about her starting her period." He kept his voice even. "I know you lived as a human in a culture that treated... fertility like a supernatural power—"

"Because it is."

He nodded. "I'm not arguing that. I'm just saying that she might not see it that way. And frankly, as someone who was adopted—admittedly for different reasons than Sadia—anything involving connections to ancestors is really complicated. The feelings are really hard to sort through."

"So avoiding those feelings is preferable to examining them with her great-grandmother, her older brother, and other people who love and care for her?"

"Fuck." He sank into a sofa near the brick fireplace. "Dammit."

"Are you cursing because you know I'm correct?"

His jaw was tense. "Maybe."

Tenzin floated over and straddled him, settling onto his legs and combing her fingers through the dark curls that grew longer each year. "We love Sadia. We celebrate the day of her birth and her achievements in education and athletics. She should be celebrated for who she is and who she is becoming, Benjamin. Who else would be better than us to show her that everything about her is honorable and good and worthy of commemoration?"

He thought about it for a long time, then let out a long sigh. "Am I going to have to learn a dance?"

"I don't know, but I'd like you to remain open to the idea."

NINE

Audley Manor was a vast and sprawling house
with a large central courtyard. Formal rooms
were contained on the first floor, along with
the massive library that spread through the entire north
wing of the house. Over the library on the second floor
were the servants' quarters, and on the south side of the
house, the lavish bedrooms for the Mortimer family and
formal rooms downstairs.

Beatrice crept up the stairs on catlike feet, silently
casting her amnis into the darkness to gauge the threat
she was facing.

Amnis was a tricky thing to manage. The energy that
lived under her skin kept her alive, animated her, gave her
power over her body and her element. It could also give
her away to another vampire with good senses.

When Beatrice reached the top of the stairs that led to
the servants' quarters, she paused. She felt two vampires
in the general vicinity, but they were moving quickly

toward the south wing and the family quarters, no doubt searching for anything that could be a hiding place or a safe.

Something tickled the back of her mind, but it was ephemeral and fleeting.

She sensed four humans in the south wing and knew that at least two of them would be Mrs. Dawson, the housekeeper; and Barnes, the mysterious butler they'd never met.

Was it Barnes who had planned all this? A servant's revenge on an ungrateful master? An attempt to avenge a real or imagined wrong?

Beatrice caught a whiff of cologne and headed right. It was an unfamiliar scent that stood out in the musty air of the old stone house.

Were the humans or the vampires more dangerous? It was impossible to tell. She went for the nearest threat.

Slipping into the bedroom where she smelled the cologne, Beatrice saw a figure sleeping under a large mound of blankets. There was a cup of tea cooling on the nightstand, a pair of round reading glasses, and two large hearing aids sitting next to them.

Mrs. Dawson was white-haired and peaceful when she slept, and a massive snore told Beatrice she hadn't been disturbed in the least by the intruder in her room.

Across the room, a dark figure was looking into a built-in closet. Beatrice crept up to him and tapped him on the shoulder.

The man spun, his eyes going wide.

"Good thing she needs those hearing aids, huh?"

Beatrice didn't wait but punched the man in the face, knocking his head back with a satisfying thwack. There was a snap and a crunching sound; then the scent of blood poured into her nostrils, sweet and tempting.

The man covered his bloody nose with his left hand but lunged forward, a hunting knife in his right. He swiped out clumsily, and Beatrice ducked back. He missed her by inches.

"Now now," she whispered. "Rude." She grabbed his wrist and twisted; the knife fell with a thunk to the floor.

The heavy boom seemed to echo in the silent house and Beatrice froze.

The man froze.

Mrs. Dawson's snore paused, then immediately started up again.

The man twisted out of her grip and rolled away from her, crouching down and scrambling for the knife on the ground.

"I don't have time for this," she hissed. "What's the plan?"

She grabbed for the stranger in black, who knocked a floor lamp into a heavy set of drapes, then hooked her arm around his neck and dug her fingers into his skin, intending to make him talk, but her amnis came on too strong. He slumped in her arms, dead asleep.

"Shit."

Beatrice closed the closet door, set the lamp back on its base, and kicked the hunting knife under the bed as she dragged the unconscious human out of the room. She'd have to get the knife later.

Mrs. Dawson kept snoring.

S he locked the unconscious human in the bathroom, grateful for old doors and skeleton keys that worked from the outside, then hunted down the next human. He was going through a massive linen room next to the bath, tearing through the drawers and cupboards with so much concentration that she came up behind him and put him to sleep in seconds.

That left the mysterious Barnes, Elise, and one more human unaccounted for, along with the two vampires she could hear in the attic overhead.

Were they looking for a safe? A treasure room? Beatrice had a feeling that whatever Lord Mortimer might have taken, it was probably smaller than what these opportunists were thinking. In her experience, most vampires kept their treasure caches small, portable, and easy to hide.

Of course, the cache of treasure had been in a remote region of Central Asia, hardly a place where a vampire would expect humans to stumble on it.

Gold.

Idols.

Ceremonial weapons.

Jewels.

With a description that vague, the treasure could have been the size of a room or as small as an ice chest. Would

Lord Mortimer keep something that valuable around the family quarters? Near the bedrooms where his nieces and nephews slept?

She walked to the south wing of the house where Elise was sleeping, but all the bedrooms were empty. Had she heard the intruders and gone downstairs to look for Nick? Were human police already on the way?

A quick scan of the second floor proved no one other than Mrs. Dawson was there, and she no longer heard vampires above her. Where had they gone?

She heard something crash below her.

Rushing down the stairs in the south wing of the house, she raced through a ballroom, a formal parlor, a drawing room, and a smoking room before she managed to find a hallway that she recognized. She flung her senses wide, searching for the vampires she knew had to be lurking on the first floor.

She felt them in minutes, and they were in the worst place imaginable.

The library.

Beatrice rushed into the palace of books, only to freeze when she saw the scene in front of her.

René, bleeding from the throat and held at knifepoint by a tall, male vampire with dark hair, dripping fangs, and a unibrow that defied modern grooming. Another vampire held René's shoulders from the back, keeping him motionless.

"Beatrice." René kept his eyes on her. "It seems we have visitors."

His voice might have been calm, but the rage was seething below the surface.

She wondered why he didn't simply break free since neither vampire seemed to have a firm hold on him, until she realized that the knife wasn't at his neck but *in* it, the tip of the blade likely brushing his spine.

"Everyone stay calm." She raised both her hands. "Your men are alive upstairs. Everyone is alive down here. No one needs to get hurt."

A burley human in a ski mask held an older man that Beatrice assumed was the mysterious Barnes. He was dressed in an old-fashioned pair of pin-striped pajamas, and his hair was mussed, probably from being dragged out of bed.

Beatrice smiled at him. "Mr. Barnes, I'm guessing?"

"You must be Miss De Novo," the dignified man said. "I apologize for making your acquaintance like this."

"No apologies necessary." Beatrice finally turned to the dark-haired Elise, who was holding Nick at gunpoint, wearing a black bodysuit and half a smile.

"Madame Vampire," the woman said. "So nice to meet you properly."

"Always a pleasure, Elise."

"Don't call her that," René spat out. "Her real name is Emilie."

TEN

"Hardly my real name," Elise said. "Just the one you gave me when I was your apprentice."

Nick was pale and blinking like a deer caught in headlights. "I am so confused. Elise, what is happening?"

Beatrice was definitely going to wipe the poor man's memory after this. He looked moments away from a heart attack.

"Nick, I promise I will explain everything when we figure out what these people want." Beatrice sent her amnis out, but she sensed no other threats. Elise had two vampire accomplices and the human holding Barnes.

She could take all four of them herself, but the human hostages gave her pause. Humans were fragile. Also, Beatrice really didn't want to have to explain to Gemma why her nephew was missing his head.

Her options were limited. There was no water in the library, so her elemental power was muted. She didn't want anyone dying, and she also hated the idea of blood getting on the books. Blood was impossible to get out of old paper and vellum.

"This was all very nicely played." Beatrice spoke to Elise, trying to defuse the tension in the room. "How long were you and Nick engaged?"

"Two years," she said. "I've known about the Mortimer treasure for far longer, of course. I heard about it from René."

She cut her eyes at him. "I knew you were lying. Who are you really working for?"

"Uh..." René looked away.

Elise was more direct. "Arosh."

Beatrice's eyes went wide. "You willingly went to work for the Fire King of Central Asia?"

Elise smirked. "He pays well."

"I hope so."

"Arosh has numerous gold caches, but he wants this one returned."

"And his journal," René added. "I wasn't lying about that."

Beatrice rolled her eyes. "Oh no, you've been totally up front."

"The book is not technically part of the treasure." René skipped his habitual shrug since it would have meant a knife in his spine. "I was helping you and helping myself. There was no need to burden you with information unnecessary for the job. And if I happened to find information about the treasure, you had no reason to know it."

Elise looked at Beatrice but kept the gun on Nick. "You had to know he was lying to you. That's what he does. He lies."

René whispered something in French that Beatrice didn't catch.

"Shut up," Elise said. "That doesn't work on me anymore."

"Okay, I'll bite." Beatrice saw the woman getting more and more agitated. "Where's the Mortimer treasure? It's not in the attic. Your friends searched there. It's not anywhere on the second floor. Nothing but bedrooms and family rooms up there."

"It's in the library of course." Elise nodded over Beatrice's shoulder. "I'm surprised the renowned book detective missed such an obvious clue."

Beatrice glanced over her shoulder for a second, catching the portrait of Penelope and Charles over the fireplace. She pictured it in her mind, examining the details that she'd admired when she first saw it.

"I think they had it painted here. Under that stained glass window."

"Why do you say that?"

"There's a slightly rosy tint... During the day, that's where the sun hits."

"No, there's a door in that picture and there's not one on the wall."

"They could have moved it."

"Moved a door in a place like this?"

Beatrice smiled. "They didn't move the door. They covered it."

René murmured, "The mudroom."

It was small because Lord Mortimer had turned part of it into a treasure room. Who would look for treasure sandwiched between a library of old books and a mudroom with rickety hunting gear?

"Dear Lord," Nick said. "Is that why that mudroom is such a mess? I told Aunt Penny a hundred times that we needed to expand it, but she always—"

"Shut up." Elise jammed the gun in Nick's ribs. "You and your stupid family. Your ridiculous traditions and titles."

Nick was clearly scared, but his face fell. "I thought you loved me."

Elise muttered something in French that Beatrice also didn't hear, but René's eyes only grew more stormy.

"The bookcase swings out," Elise said. "I can reach the door, but I can't open it. What is the combination?"

"You expect me to know?" Nick's eyes went wide. "I didn't even know there was a safe in the mudroom."

"A vault," Elise hissed. "And you expect me to believe the Mortimer heir doesn't know anything about the Mortimer treasure? That they would pass this house to you and not tell you where to find the real source of your wealth?" Her voice rose. "Do you think I'm an idiot?"

Nick was sweating, which made his blood pump harder and his scent rise. Beatrice saw the two vampires holding René turn toward him, their instincts drawn to the lure of prey. One already had his fangs out, and the other's eyes were fixed on the panicking human.

Beatrice quickly calculated how she could protect

Nick and Barnes, who were the only truly innocent people in the room. René would have to fend for himself.

The human holding Barnes didn't have a weapon, and his compatriots upstairs had been easily taken down. Beatrice could rush Elise and knock the gun out of her hand, but unfortunately, the chance of her shooting Nick at close range was high.

De-escalate. It was the only option to keep everyone alive.

"Tell me the combination." Elise was losing patience. "I've wasted two years of my life in this ridiculous village. Tell me now!"

Nick's voice was desperate. "Elise, I don't know it. I don't know about any vault."

"Liar. Your aunt told you everything."

"Not... everything." Barnes's voice was a balm on the swiftly escalating situation. He looked at Beatrice. "Not nearly everything."

Elise turned the gun on Barnes. "You."

"The earl passed quite unexpectedly, you see." Barnes glanced at Nick but kept his eyes on the gun. "He did intend to tell you, but of course he hadn't expected to die until you were old enough to know. And he wasn't particularly proud of what he'd done."

"Barnes?" Nick frowned. "What are you saying?"

"Your father.... His Lordship loved him very much, but he had quite expensive tastes. The earl didn't trust your father or your aunt to do the right thing, but he'd hoped that you might return some of the more culturally important things in time. The gold, of course, would have been up to you."

"Merde." René blinked. "The old man knew about it all?"

Nick frowned. "You're saying Elise is right? That there is actually a vault of treasure here in the library?"

Beatrice wanted to point out that gold and historic weapons really couldn't compare to the vast wealth of a properly curated library, but she had a feeling it wasn't the time.

"You." Elise shoved Nick at the burly man holding Barnes. "Take him."

Beatrice immediately calculated how she'd take out the human in the black mask, but that still left Barnes with Elise's gun on him.

"Take me to the vault." She put the muzzle in Barnes's back and shoved the old man toward the far wall. "Open the safe and we'll leave you alive."

René caught Beatrice's eye, but she shook her head slightly. She didn't want to risk Barnes getting shot.

"Wait." Elise kept the gun on Barnes and looked at Beatrice. "The vampire goes first. Then René and my men, then Nick, then me."

Dammit. The minute the woman's back was to Beatrice, she'd been thinking she could get her hands on her and flood her system with amnis to knock her out.

The woman wasn't dumb.

They dutifully lined up in the order Elise had stated. The vampires holding René waited for Beatrice to walk in front of them, then Nick and the henchman followed with Elise holding Barnes at gunpoint and bringing up the rear. They marched down the center of the library toward the bookcases that lined the far wall.

They fanned out to the side while Barnes pulled a dummy book from the middle of the shelf. Beatrice heard a soft click, and the old bookcase swung out from the wall. The hinges moved in silence, revealing a simple metal door with an electronic lock and a large wheel with a combination in the center.

"It looks like a bank vault," Nick said.

"It's similar." Barnes bent over and began to enter the combination, which led to a heavy-sounding metallic clunk from somewhere behind the door. Then he began to spin the wheel in a pattern Beatrice quickly memorized. Moments later, Beatrice heard another click and the metal door unsealed.

"Lord Mortimer." Barnes pulled back the door. "The Mortimer vault."

"Bonfire."

"Yes."

"Dancing."

"Maybe."

"A goat."

Ben put down the pen he was using to take notes. "No. For the last time, we are not getting 'just a small goat' to butcher for Sadia's... whatever this is."

"Coming-of-age ritual."

"Coming of— Tenzin, have you actually talked to Sadia about any of this?" He rubbed his temple. He knew he was a vampire and vampires didn't get headaches unless they were deprived of blood for too long and their bodies began to go into stasis, but this entire conversation was making him remember headaches.

For good reason.

"It's not her job to plan her own party." Tenzin was floating over the bed, braiding colored thread into a strand of hair that was hanging in front of her. "She has enough going on; she doesn't need that kind of pressure."

"But we are planning a ceremony for her, trying to recognize her culture and link to her ancestors, and you're not asking her about it."

Tenzin settled on the bed. "You're right. We should ask Dema what a traditional Syrian coming-of-age ceremony would look like."

Dema wasn't as helpful as Ben had hoped.

"Seriously?" Dema raised an eyebrow. "I grew up in Southern California. All I wanted was a drivers' license and a car when I became a teenager."

"What about Syrian Muslim traditions?"

"Sadia is Syrian but not Muslim. Her birth parents were Orthodox and her adoptive parents are Catholic. And I don't think there's any kind of Christian *or*

Muslim coming-of-age ceremony in Syria when you hit puberty." Dema shrugged. "I didn't have one. About the only thing that kind of marked that time was I decided I wanted to wear a hijab." She touched the edge of her headscarf. "And that was mostly because my older sisters *didn't* wear it."

"Really?"

"Yeah, my parents left it up to us. And I was the youngest, so I wanted to be different. Plus my boobs grew right around that time and I felt self-conscious."

Tenzin cocked her head. "You felt self-conscious about your breasts?" She looked at them. "They're not particularly sizable."

Ben bit his lip to keep from laughing.

"Thanks." Dema's expression didn't change. "They weren't big, but I was like the first girl in my class that had to wear a bra and I hated it." She shrugged. "I felt like the hijab made people take me more seriously. It made me feel grown-up."

Tenzin nodded carefully. "What do you think would make Sadia feel grown-up?"

Ben sat up straight. "Actually, that's a really good question."

"Don't sound surprised," Tenzin said. "I have a lot of them because I'm much older than you."

Dema took a long breath and let it out slowly. "You know, she's already mature for her age, so the main thing I'd say she struggles with is feeling out of place at school. She's just not the typical twelve-year-old."

"You think she'd want a party or something? With her

friends?" Ben wouldn't have pegged his little sister for a party animal.

"No," Dema continued. "I think she takes pride in being different. Whatever you do, don't play into any teenage-girl stereotypes. In fact, I'd say the stranger the better."

Tenzin's eyes lit up. "Make it weird?"

Dema nodded. "Yeah. The weirder the better. She's her mother's daughter whether she wants to admit it or not. Find some ancient coming-of-age tradition that no one has practiced in a thousand years or something and she'll probably think it's cool. Especially if blood is involved."

"God help me," Ben muttered.

ELEVEN

The heavy metal door that opened led to another wooden door like the one portrayed in the painting.

"For God's sake, open it," Elise said, still holding the gun to Barnes's ribs.

He stepped forward and pulled the large brass knob, but the room beyond was cloaked in darkness.

"There is a light switch just inside on the right wall." Barnes straightened his shoulders.

"So turn it on."

The old man stepped into the darkness, and a second later, the light turned on.

Beatrice could see paintings hanging on the walls.

"Okay, everyone in!" Elise motioned to the vampires holding René, then at Beatrice. "Same order. Vampires first."

As Beatrice walked into the vault, she heard Barnes speak.

"Take what you will, but the young earl knew nothing of any of this. I beg you to leave him unharmed."

"And you, old man? You never liked me."

"I admit I had my reservations about you, and clearly they have been proven correct."

Beatrice walked to the far wall of the Mortimer vault and turned, keeping her hands visible.

They're going to lock us in.

Beatrice was nearly sure of it, and she felt a spike of fear when she realized that once the bookcases were back in place, their prison would be completely concealed.

You're a mated vampire, B. Giovanni will find you.

Relief flooded her. Elise might make off with Arosh's treasure, but she couldn't blame the woman for that. As long as Elise remained calm and the gun didn't go off, as long as the knife at René's spine didn't move, Giovanni would find them, she could wipe Nick's memory, and everything would be fine.

"Barnes!" Nick hissed. "Don't antagonize her. Elise, this is madness. Why are you working for someone called a fire king? What is all this, and why are those men...?" He was finally registering that the men holding René were not simple thugs. "My God, this is barbaric. You must let us go."

One of the vampires holding René curled his lip at Nick, revealing a long, gleaming white fang.

Nick took one shaky breath, and then his eyes rolled back and he fainted, falling to the stone floor of the vault.

Elise began cursing in French. "This weakling. Leave him, Bertrand."

The thug moved his full attention to Barnes, who was standing calmly in the threshold of the vault door, the gun still trained on him.

Barnes stepped toward Nick. "Miss Elise, please don't hurt the earl. There has been no wrong done to you. He has done nothing but show you consideration and love."

The corner of Elise's mouth twitched. "He didn't even know me, Barnes."

She spat out a stream of rapid French faster than Beatrice could follow; then one of the vampires holding René sped away.

Beatrice was watching everyone, looking for the best way to defuse the situation, keep the humans alive, and escape the vault she was now standing in.

Usually she enjoyed a good vault, but not when guns were involved.

"What's the plan?" Beatrice asked. "Just want to know what to expect."

"When Mario gets back," Elise said, "you can help him pack the treasure. Like I said, if you cooperate, everyone stays alive." She looked at Nick's unconscious body. "Bertrand, get him out of the way."

Beatrice kept her attention on Elise as the other human dragged an unconscious Nick against the wall.

Despite their precarious circumstances, Beatrice couldn't help but marvel at the Mortimer vault. "Impressive." She glanced at Barnes. "It's all from one cache in the Khyber Pass?"

There were gold leaf frames on the walls, surrounding intricately painted classical works of Persian art. There was a large stack of old gold bars and a sizable chest of silver coins. There were gold lamps and ceremonial weapons hanging in a rack on one wall along with a glass pitcher of what looked like uncut gemstones.

There was also a bookcase of manuscripts and scrolls carefully packaged that made Beatrice yearn to ignore the health of the human hostages and let loose an attack that would level the intruders, but she resisted.

At the end of the day, what did she care if Arosh hired someone to retrieve his own treasure? She couldn't blame him; he'd probably been fending off archeologists for years.

"Not all of it is from the cache, but most of it. They found it in the mountains." Barnes's voice was quiet. "It was in a very remote region and was quite hidden."

I bet.

Arosh was one of the most ancient vampires on earth. No doubt he had caches all over Central Asia and forgot about them all the time.

Just her luck he'd happened to remember this one.

Barnes continued. "They took the treasure back with them and divided it between the men. This is only a small portion of the total cache."

Beatrice was even more impressed.

"Wait." Elise looked around. "But where is the rest?"

Barnes frowned. "What do you mean?"

"My employer told me to expect ten times this amount of gold." She pointed the gun at Barnes's face. "Where is the rest?"

Beatrice felt the tension rise. Elise was losing control

of her emotions. "Didn't you hear what Barnes just said? They split the treasure among the men who discovered it." She gestured to the art on the walls, the gold, and the weapons. "This is more than enough to prove to Arosh that you are making progress. Take this and explain you're still searching for the rest."

"Fuck you!"

"Listen." Beatrice's fangs fell at the insult, but she took a calming breath and tried to reason with the young woman. "I'm the most dangerous vampire here." She glanced at the immortal holding René. "My sire was Tenzin's mate; I'm not trying to brag, but I know you've heard of Tenzin."

The vampire holding René muttered something indistinguishable.

Beatrice continued. "I'm not going to fight you over Arosh's treasure. As far as I'm concerned, he has every right to send someone to retrieve it. I'm only concerned that everyone leaves this situation alive." She held out her hands. "The vault is yours. Let me take Nick, Barnes, and René, and we'll be gone."

They'd have to retrieve the sleeping Mrs. Dawson from upstairs, but that wouldn't be difficult.

Elise laughed. "You're fooling yourself if you think I would trust a vampire. I know the type René works with." She glanced at the vampire holding her former mentor, and her eyes filled with emotion. "I'm sorry, René. In the end, I am sorry it turned out this way."

René scoffed. "No, you're not."

She smirked. "Fine. I'm not, but it was good to return

to the crying damsel in distress for a moment, wasn't it? That ploy always worked so well."

A crying damsel? Beatrice narrowed her eyes.

Barnes stumbled and distracted her.

"Mr. Barnes?" Beatrice stepped toward him.

"Ah ah." Elise moved the gun closer.

The man looked pale, and sweat poured from his temples. "The earl... is injured."

Nick hadn't woken, but he didn't seem to be harmed. He was crumpled in the corner with a red lump rising on his temple.

"Nick is going to be fine." Beatrice reassured him. "But Barnes, are you all right?"

"I don't need another fainter." Elise walked over and slapped the old man across the face. "Snap out of whatever cardiac event you're working yourself into. Shut up and sit down if you can't stand."

The old man leaned against the bookcase and closed his eyes.

Beatrice's rage burned, but the woman never moved the gun off Barnes, and she knew the elderly man could easily die from a gunshot wound.

The vampire who'd left returned with two large suitcases.

"Come on." Elise pointed at Beatrice, keeping the gun on Barnes. "Help Mario if you want your friends to survive. Bertrand, you too."

The man named Bertrand and the vampire named Mario began to pack, but the other vampire kept René in his grasp with a knife in his neck.

Beatrice helped them stuff the gold into a backpack and as many of the weapons as would fit in the suitcases, all while Elise kept the gun trained on Barnes.

Then Elise's eyes landed on the crown.

It appeared to be the crown jewel of the Mortimer vault—pun completely intended. A gold diadem that flared out at the top like a flower. The crown was inlaid with turquoise, diamonds, and a red stone that was likely carnelian. Hanging all around the crown was a veil of gold links woven in an intricate pattern.

"Careful with that one," Beatrice murmured. "Arosh is going to want it intact."

"You think I don't know that?" the young woman hissed.

Elise stared at the crown with a mix of wonder and horror, undoubtedly wondering how to pack a priceless and delicate crown into a metal suitcase without provoking the wrath of an ancient fire vampire.

Elise's hands were shaking, and she continually glanced at Nick and at Barnes. Beatrice saw the debate in her eyes. She was starting to understand the ramifications of what she was doing.

"Have you moved treasure like this before?" Beatrice asked, still placing gold bricks into the backpack.

"Yes, of course I have."

She hadn't. It was evident from the slight waver in her voice.

Beatrice saw the questions whirling in her mind.

How would she get all this out of the country without being reported?

Would locking Nick and Barnes in the vault be enough?

What if someone found them before she could escape?

Elise held the crown in one hand, and the hand holding the firearm fell still.

Beatrice could see the moment that Elise decided Nick and Barnes could not be allowed to live.

And Beatrice was out of options.

The moment the gun moved from Barnes to Nick, Beatrice gripped the black backpack and lunged forward at vampire speed, using the heavy tote to knock the weapon from Elise's hand. It clattered across the stone floor but thankfully didn't discharge.

"Mario!"

The woman's immortal accomplice was nearly as fast as Beatrice.

She heard a visceral snarl behind her and grabbed for a gold-tipped spear on the wall, swinging it like a sword in the cramped room and narrowly avoiding Barnes, who ducked and toppled to the floor at René's feet. The spear collided with Mario as he sprang up toward her.

Distracted by the commotion, the vampire holding René was unprepared when the Frenchman yanked his head to the left, pulling away from the blade against his spine. The blood that the blade had stemmed poured from the gash at René's throat, filling the room with the sweet scent of blood as René and his captor began to fight.

Beatrice flung the spear into Mario's gut, lunged toward him, and twisted his neck before he could raise a hand in defense. He fell to the floor with a solid thud and lay still, but the sound of gunfire rang out and motion in the vault seemed to freeze. The scent of human blood filled her nostrils, and her fangs dropped again.

Elise was standing over Barnes's prone body, her face spattered with blood and her hands shaking. Her eyes were wide when she pointed the gun at the vampire fighting René.

"Leave him." She shifted the firearm and pulled the trigger without another word.

"No!"

René fell to the floor, blood pouring from the hollow at the base of his throat.

"Get the gold," the woman said. "We'll lock them in."

Before Beatrice could stop them, the nameless vampire grabbed the backpack of gold, Elise snatched the priceless gold crown, and both of them fled from the vault, the human Bertrand following behind, dragging one of the two suitcases packed with treasure.

A fraction of a second later, the door slammed shut and Beatrice heard the combination lock spinning to secure the vault.

She turned and saw René and Barnes both on the ground bleeding while Nick and the vampire she'd been fighting lay motionless at her feet.

Beatrice looked around the vault, searching for another exit, but she saw nothing.

We're locked in a secret vault in a castle in the middle of nowhere.

"Beatrice?"

"René!" She ran over and crouched down. "Are you okay?"

He was moving, so the bullet hadn't hit his spine.

"It burns like fire." He coughed up a stream of blood. "But I'll survive. The bullet went through. It's a flesh wound only."

Both of them turned to Barnes.

"The old man is losing a lot of blood." René bit into his arm and tore at his own flesh, letting a stream of vampire blood drip from his wrist. "I'm going to try to stop the bleeding, but he needs a human doctor." He turned his eyes to her. "You're the genius. Find a way out."

Beatrice should have stopped all this before they even got to the vault. She'd been avoiding gunfire, and it had happened anyway. Now Barnes was bleeding out and they were locked in a stone vault.

Giovanni would come. He would discover them.

But would he be too late for Barnes?

TWELVE

Giovanni's driver reached the edge of Hereford, and a wave of fear hit Giovanni in the throat.

His mate was in trouble.

"Drive faster!" he yelled at the man in the front seat. "There's an emergency at Audley."

"Yes, sir." The man wasn't just a chauffeur—he was one of Terry's drivers, which meant that speed was not a problem.

Would that I were a wind vampire.

It wouldn't be the first time Giovanni had rued the day he'd been sired to fire. Granted, being a water vampire in this situation would have been equally useless. He wished Tenzin or Benjamin was at his side.

The punch of adrenaline sent his system into overdrive. His fangs lengthened and his body heated up. He consciously tamped down the urge to ignite, knowing that setting his car on fire wouldn't get him to Beatrice any faster.

What had gone wrong?

The car raced toward the manor house, crossing snowy lanes and narrow bridges, twisting and turning along the rural country roads.

Was it René? Had the Frenchman double-crossed them?

"Vehicle approaching from Audley," the driver said. "Block the road?"

"How far are we?" Beatrice's emotions had calmed down to a steady tension over the past few minutes before punching up into a near panic a moment ago.

"We're nearing the property, sir. Nothing much would come down this road unless it was coming from Audley Manor."

"Block it."

It was too much of a coincidence for a car to be leaving Audley Manor in the middle of the night just as Beatrice's emotions were this high.

He knew his mate could handle nearly anything thrown at her, but there were vulnerable humans at the manor and she would think of their safety before her own.

The car swerved to block the road, and at the same time, Giovanni yanked the door of the old Range Rover open, flinging himself into the night.

He flicked the lighter he kept in his pocket and brought a ball of blue fire to his palm, coaxing it larger and larger before he flung it at the hood of the oncoming vehicle—a dark-colored cargo van—which hit the brakes, but not before the fire engulfed the front bumper and spread up the windshield.

He urged the fire with his amnis, forcing it up and over the roof of the van and along the sides. He didn't let it encroach into the car; he wanted the driver and occupants to get out.

"Help!" A young woman with dark hair escaped from the driver's door and ran toward them, holding her arms out. "Help me, he's a monster!"

She ran to the middle of the road and stopped, panting as she kept one eye on him and glanced back at the van. "Help me!"

Oh, she was clever. A good actress. A shame that she was lying through her pretty red lips. "Miss Lambert? Elise Lambert?"

She blinked tears from her eyes and sniffed. "Wh-who are you?" She looked at the driver, who'd left the vehicle and was standing at the ready, his hand ready to draw a weapon. "What's going on? Can you call the police?"

"I don't think you want us to call the police." Giovanni glanced at the van where flames were flickering with a low blue light. "Do you, Miss Lambert?"

"Do I know you?" She turned to Terry's driver. "I'm so confused. What's going on?"

"She been touched by the amnis, sir?"

Elise played the confused damsel. "The what? What's he talking about?"

A vampire stumbled from the other side of the van with a bleeding temple and a baffled expression. He spotted Giovanni immediately, and his vision cleared. He glanced at the fire, then back to Giovanni.

"My name is Giovanni di Spada," he said quietly. "I think you've heard of me."

The vampire bared his fangs, turned, and fled into the night. A few seconds later, another human kicked out the back of the van and ran after the vampire.

Giovanni turned to Elise. *You should be running too.*

The crying woman let out a sob and ran toward Terry's driver, the only other human left. "Oh my God, can you help me? He took me and made me drive—I don't know what happened! I'm so confused and I don't remember—"

"Miss, calm down now." Terry's driver frowned. "Sir, what do you want to do? I think she was a hostage."

Beatrice was still panicking, and Giovanni knew that whatever had happened that night, a human was likely hurt, possibly dead. "Call a doctor. Someone from Graves Court. Have them sent to Audley immediately."

"T-to Audley?" Elise sniffed, but her eyes turned calculating. "Where is Graves Court? Is that where you're going? Can you take me? I want to speak to the police."

No doubt to spin a very fine tale, maybe one worthy of Shakespeare's pen.

The driver looked at Giovanni.

He smiled. "Yes, take Miss Lambert to Graves Court, but search her for weapons first. That vampire had a bullet wound."

All semblance of fear fell from Elise's eyes, and she bolted.

Not before Giovanni could catch her.

"Let me go!"

He grabbed one wrist, then the other, holding her without damaging her despite what his instincts would have preferred. "I knew who you were before we even arrived, Miss Lambert. I'll use that name since it appears you've done quite a good job building that identity."

Elise stopped struggling and looked up. "Who are you?"

"You just heard me refer to myself as Giovanni di Spada, but that's a name I don't go by very often anymore. These days I go by Giovanni Vecchio."

The blood drained from her face.

"Sound familiar? You might know me as Ben Vecchio's uncle... Emilie."

THIRTEEN

Beatrice was searching the back of the door with no success. "There has to be a latch. No one designs a vault that can't be opened from the inside in case of emergency."

"It's been five minutes." René was holding his throat, but the blood loss had already stopped and his voice was clear again. "How hard can an old library door be?"

She stepped back to look at the door thorough the eyes of a safe designer. There were three points where she would have hidden a safety latch, and none of them held anything but stone. "Maybe along the base?" She crouched down and felt along the wooden door. "This door must be two inches thick of solid oak."

"Keep in mind" —René was holding a wad of torn cotton from his shirt to the bullet wound in Barnes's gut — "we're not talking about master thieves here. They probably didn't foresee a con artist in league with vampires maneuvering her way into the heart of the

Mortimer heir, then robbing them blind and shooting their butler. Merde! How hard is it to open a door?"

"I'm a water vampire and a librarian!" She lost her patience and turned to him. "Do you see any water? Do you see a code or a puzzle to solve? You're the earth vampire here! We're surrounded by stone. *You* do something, Du Pont."

"Hold this!" He waited for Beatrice to come over and keep pressure on Barnes's wound. "His heartbeat is slow but stable."

"I've been listening." She carefully placed pressure on the wound while trying not to hurt the old man.

René's color was back to normal, and he looked as hearty as he had before the shooting. Beatrice more than half wondered if he'd taken a sip from the unconscious earl when her back was turned.

"Barnes is older, but he's healthy."

"Thank Christ."

"Giovanni will be able to find us," Beatrice said. "One of the advantages of being mated—"

"Yes, yes, yes." René rolled his eyes. "His blood calls to yours and yours to his. I've heard the stories. Just shut up and keep the old man alive."

Beatrice wanted to strangle him, but she bit her tongue instead. If he could do anything to move the stones of the door without bringing the entire vault and the manor above it crashing down, she'd swallow every threat she'd ever made against the arrogant vampire.

"I don't have a fraction of my grandsire's strength."

René put his hands on the metal hinges. "But I do take after him in one way."

Earth vampires were funny creatures. Maybe the most nonvampiric of their kind, they tended to be associated with home, hearth, and family. They had sprawling clans and avoided drama if they weren't René du Pont.

They also had different affinities, some for stone, some for living things, and others...

The metal under René's hands began to warp.

Yes. Thank God, finally a stroke of luck. René's affinity was to metal.

"These hinges are old iron," René said. "And heavy. If they were newer, they'd be easier to warp."

"And the metal door outside?"

"I should be able to break that one easily. Modern metal isn't as dense as the older kind."

She watched him slowly pry the iron hinges from the door. "Is this how you've escaped from prison so many times?"

He glanced over his shoulder. "Where did you hear that?"

"From your aunt. I think she's proud of you."

"Heh." René humphed. "She could show it better."

"She's saved your life a half dozen times at least."

"She married that Neanderthal with no fashion sense. *She* should be running London, not him."

It was Beatrice's turn to roll her eyes.

She heard Nick stirring. Without missing a beat, she reached over and sent him right back to sleep with her amnis. The last thing she needed was another panicking human.

"Miss De Novo."

Barnes was conscious. Barely.

"Mr. Barnes, we're working on getting out of here. We've stabilized the wound, and the bleeding has slowed down. We're going to get you to a—"

"Is Lord Mortimer safe?"

Beatrice sighed. "He's fine, Mr. Barnes. Please don't worry about Nick. He's strong and he'll be okay."

"I believe Mrs. Dawson is also safe. Did I hear you say that?"

She might be waking up to a couple of thieves shouting through duct tape, but Beatrice was relatively certain they were well and thoroughly trapped in the broom closet. "I believe she's safe too."

"Miss Lambert—"

"Is gone. I'm sure..." She felt a wave of warmth pass through her. "My husband is almost here. I can feel him."

"Good." René grunted. "These hinges are ancient."

"This room is as old as the house itself," Barnes said. "It originally led directly to the mudroom." He looked at the back wall. "It was bricked up to create the vault."

The feelings from Giovanni were confused, so Beatrice took a deep breath. She didn't need him blazing into the house and setting everything on fire. The most important thing was to get Barnes help.

"Is there another way into the mudroom from here?" Beatrice asked.

Barnes shook his head. "We didn't think... I suppose we didn't plan well, did we?"

"It's a beautiful little vault, Mr. Barnes. Very safe from... everyone." Beatrice scanned the room, looking at the art that was left, the bookcases of manuscripts and scrolls, the treasures Elise had been forced to leave behind.

"Nearly there," René said.

"How is he bending that metal?" Barnes asked. "I think Miss Lambert wasn't the only one with secrets."

"That's true," Beatrice said. "But don't worry—I'm going to wipe your memory after this so you won't remember the details."

"I'm quite sure I'll remember all this."

She muttered, "You say that now."

Giovanni was on the move again, coming closer with every breath Barnes took.

Come faster.

Help.

He needs help.

She was silently praying to all the saints when her eyes landed on the one thing that could distract her in the face of chaos. It was a crumbling old book sitting on the bookshelf, next to a pile of scrolls.

The Alchemist and other Collected Works of Ben Jonson.

She smiled a little. "Huh."

"Beatrice!"

She heard her mate's voice in the courtyard.

"We're in the library!"

"And we're free." René reached down, grabbed the

massive wooden door by the hinges, and yanked it back, revealing the grey metal door beyond with the bookcases on the other side. He put his hand to the metal around the combination lock and sank his fingers into it as if the steel was nothing more than wet cardboard. Then he pushed the door forward, snapping whatever mechanism held the bookcases in place.

"Beatrice!"

She smiled when she heard Giovanni's voice. "We need a doctor for Barnes, but everyone else is safe." She looked at René. "The Frenchman earned his share."

Elise Lambert, aka Emilie Mandel, was tied to a chair in the library of Graves Court when she woke from vampire stupor.

She murmured a string of French curses as she woke. "Arosh will kill you all."

"Not when he finds out you tried to kill my mate." Giovanni leaned forward. "And definitely not when I tell him how you nearly killed the beloved servant of a friend for no reason at all."

Elise froze when she saw Beatrice and Giovanni sitting across from her. "Where's René?"

"René who?" The growl came from a vampire sitting near the fire. He wore a pin-striped suit and his hair in a buzz cut close to his skull. His accent was anything but fine. "Welcome to Graves Court, Miss

Lambert. I'm Terrance Ramsay. Do you know who I am?"

Elise nodded.

"My friends here say that you tried to kill my neighbor and his man. Is that true?"

She shook her head. "I was defending myself in the course of a job for Arosh, the Fire King. I was retrieving his property from an English thief, and this vampire attacked me." She nodded toward Beatrice.

"Is that so?" Terry raised an eyebrow. "You're in my territory, Miss Lambert. In the employ of another vampire regent. Do I have that correct?"

She lifted her chin. "Yes."

"And did you seek permission for yourself or any of your collaborators to be in my territory on a job?" The corner of his mouth inched up. "Or did you forget that part?"

Elise said nothing.

"I know Ms. De Novo personally," Terry said. "She's not known to be a rash or violent vampire. Why would she attack you without provocation?"

The woman lifted her chin. "I work for Arosh."

"I bet you do." Terry smiled. "But I don't."

"We've already collected your human partners and delivered them to the police," Beatrice said. "They don't really know much. But you?"

Giovanni stared at her. "You're a problem."

"You said you knew who I was before you came," Elise said. "Why didn't you say anything?"

"When you first came to my attention, you were

Emilie Mandel, a minor con artist working with René du Pont who'd fooled my nephew into stealing a painting from the Metropolitan Museum of Art. You were an annoyance and a well-learned lesson, Miss Lambert, but I had no reason to track you down."

The woman lifted her chin, but added nothing to Giovanni's account.

"When you came to my attention the second time," Giovanni continued, "you were Elise Lambert who had been in a seemingly legitimate relationship with Nick Mortimer for over two years. If you'd truly turned over a new leaf, it wasn't my place to interfere with your future."

"And when René showed up?"

"Fucking little frog," Terry muttered. "If I see 'im, I swear—"

"Terry," Beatrice said. "My friend. Just a little patience. René is gone. I promise you."

He fell silent, but Giovanni could feel him brooding across the room.

"I admit that stumped me at first. Until I realized that you and René weren't working together at all. And while René had good reason to hide his presence in England, you did not." Giovanni kept his eyes on Elise. "I was cautious, but I had no idea you'd turn violent. That was my mistake. Thank God my mate was there. What was the plan before we arrived, Elise? Kill all of them and take the gold? Take the gold and simply disappear? Security was nonexistent in the library; it would have been easy."

"No one was supposed to get hurt," she spat out. "If you and your woman hadn't been there—"

"But we were," Beatrice said. "Why not wait? You had to know we'd leave eventually and then you'd be clear to break into the vault. It would have been so easy to wait. Even after Giovanni told me about you, I gave you the benefit of the doubt."

Elise pressed her lips together.

"She couldn't break in," Giovanni said. "It's exactly as she told you. She knew where the vault was located, but she didn't know the combination. And she didn't have the patience to find a thief to break into it properly. She was always going to go after the family."

Her eyes narrowed, and Giovanni knew he was right. Elise Lambert was a good actress but a poor thief. She hadn't planned well enough ahead.

"You're alive now, but we're handing you over to Terry." Giovanni sighed. "He and Gemma will decide your fate. I'm sure you wish we would call the police, but that won't happen, Elise. Emilie. Whatever your name really is. If you're lucky, Arosh might vouch for you and make restitution since a human didn't actually die."

"I myself will be making restitution to my neighbors," Terry said. "We've made sure they don't remember the worst of it, but you can bet I'll tell your boss that because of your foolishness, his treasure is back in the Mortimer vault and if he wants it, he'll need to go through me now. For that and anything else that English party took."

Elise's eyes burned with anger.

"Don't like that, do you?" Terry shrugged. "Don't much care, Miss Lambert. And the Mortimers will be getting a brand-new security system, courtesy of me."

Giovanni and Beatrice exchanged a look. Thank God they'd already secured permission from Terry to finish their search.

"Any questions for these two?" Terry asked. "Or me?"

"What are you going to do with me?" Elise asked.

"Don't know yet," Terry said. "I might hand you over to my wife." He smiled and his long fangs gleamed. "She's the mean one."

Tenzin sat down next to Sadia, who was typing on her phone.

The girl looked up. "Oh. Hey."

"Hey." Tenzin tried to copy the casual rhythm of speech she'd used. "What are you doing?"

She lifted her phone. "Just texting with Kaya."

"Your friend."

Sadia nodded. "Yeah. She's... Well, she's kind of like my sister. Neither of us has a sister—well, technically Kaya has a sister who's way older because her parents are vampires too and they adopted her big sister a long time ago, so her sister is kind of more like her aunt or something. Not like me and Ben." Sadia frowned. "It's a little like me and Ben, I guess. Technically I think Ben and Caspar are both my brothers, which is... weird."

"Vampire families are complicated."

Sadia nodded. "Yeah. But Kaya gets it. So we act like we're sisters sometimes." She laughed a little. "I know we're not, but—"

"Sisters are important. I had sisters." Tenzin hadn't remembered that in centuries. She blinked. "I had sisters."

Sadia put her phone down. "You did?"

"I did." She closed her eyes. "One older and one younger. Maybe two younger. I think one died when she was small."

"I'm sorry."

Tenzin looked up. "Don't be. That was very common. Maybe it was more common for children to die than to live then."

Sadia sank back into the sofa. "Like my family."

"Yes." Tenzin knew that most of Sadia's family were dead. Other than a few cousins on her mother's side, Giovanni had found death records for most of the girl's extended family. "But you're not dead. You're very much alive. You survived. You must not ever feel guilty, because the fact that you survived means that all of them also survived."

Sadia frowned. "I've never thought of it that way before."

"Humans now are very frightened to talk about death, but it's the one thing that all mortals experience." Tenzin frowned. "Unless they become a vampire."

"Like I will."

Tenzin cocked her head. "Will you?" She'd long

suspected that the girl would choose immortality. Very few humans were as suited to immortal life as Sadia.

"Yes." Sadia heaved a great sigh. "But I know that it's not for a very long time, and Dad always reminds me that my frontal cortex isn't fully developed until age twenty-five, so I can't make any permanent decisions until after that anyway."

Had Tenzin's frontal cortex been undeveloped when she was turned?

That would probably explain a few things.

"You can't decide that right now," Tenzin said. "But I have sensed something that you should be aware of so you can make plans."

Sadia's eyes went wide. "Can you really tell the future? Dad says you can't and Mom says you can."

"I can tell this future: you will be starting to menstruate within the next week."

The girl's expression froze. "Tenzin, ew."

"There is nothing 'ew' about it. It's very evident from your scent. This is a thing that must be celebrated, so I want you to—"

"Oh my God, can Ben tell that I'm about to start my period too?"

Tenzin blinked. "He probably doesn't realize the subtle changes in hormonal scent—"

"Oh my God." She covered her face. "I have to tell Kaya. She's around vampires everywhere, and she would absolutely die."

Tenzin thought for a moment. "You mean die in a figurative sense, correct?"

"Yes, Tenzin. Oh my God!"

"Okay." She raised a hand to calm the girl. "It's fine. I'm sure Kaya's parents will have informed her about this biological reality, but if you feel you must text her, I do not object. In fact, you might invite her to your ceremony."

Ben had drilled into Tenzin that calling it a fertility rite would probably panic the girl, so they'd decided to call it a ceremony.

Sadia frowned. "What ceremony? You want to have a ceremony for my *period*?"

"I want to have a ceremony to celebrate your... maturity." Tenzin angled herself toward Sadia. "You are alive. Despite everything you went through, you are alive and you are approaching adulthood."

Sadia looked away. "Everyone does that."

"No." Tenzin reached for the girl's hand and held it firmly. "Not everyone."

Sadia was silent for a long time.

"When we celebrate these things," Tenzin continued, "it may seem strange to you. Or foreign because this modern culture takes life for granted."

Sadia met Tenzin's eyes. "But we don't."

Tenzin shook her head. "No, we do not."

The girl blinked, and Tenzin could see her interest piqued.

"Well..." She sat up. "What would a ceremony be like?"

"When I was your age, my parents slaughtered a goat

and held a bonfire and there was a lot of dancing and I received my first tattoos."

Sadia opened her mouth. Then closed it.

Heaven above, she looked like a fish. Just like Ben.

"Okay, I definitely don't want to slaughter a goat," Sadia said. "And I'm not much of a dancer, but I do like bonfires and I definitely want tattoos. My parents would probably freak out about tattoos, though. Any other ideas?"

Excellent. It was exactly what Tenzin had been hoping for. "Am I correct in believing you were born in Aleppo?"

"Yes."

"Then I have several ideas associated with Ḥepat, the storm goddess of ancient Aleppo. The ceremony would involve rainwater, gold and silver objects, and possibly a leopard."

"I am so in."

FOURTEEN

Giovanni, Beatrice, and René du Pont gathered around the large, leather-bound copy of Ben Jonson's collected works, staring at the book that had been hidden in the Mortimer vault along with various priceless scrolls and manuscripts. Next to it was the leather-bound volume that Giovanni's old friend, Edward Macintosh, had rebound for Penny before her death.

The Alchemist. 1612. A DRAMATIC PLAY BY BEN JONSON.

The Alchemist and Other Collected Works of Ben Jonson.

One was a beautiful, gold-detailed book that looked like a work of art. The other was a crumbling, leather-bound relic that nearly fell apart in Giovanni's hands.

"What would you estimate?" Beatrice asked.

Giovanni picked up the leather-bound relic. "The volume Edward rebound is undoubtedly more valuable for the craft alone. The leatherwork and the binding have been completely redone. The pages of the book are intact and readable."

"And yet the crumbling one was kept in the vault," René added.

Giovanni carefully set it down. "If the play is hidden anywhere, I suspect Penny hid it in the pages of this thing."

René's eyebrows flew up. "*If?* You coerce me into being your ally to find a treasure you're not even sure of?" More muttered French curses. "And for this I have angered Arosh by losing the chance to find his own journal."

Giovanni pointed at a brown box on the next table. "Don't be absurd. I found Arosh's journal before I left for London. Edward cleaned it and tightened the binding before I left town. You can deliver it to him with a clear conscience."

René stared at Giovanni with suspicion. "Why?"

Giovanni shrugged. "I hold to my promises, Du Pont. You could learn from that."

He looked at Beatrice. "But Elise—"

"You're not responsible for Elise," Beatrice said. "Are you?"

The vampire cocked his head. "No, I am not. Arosh hired her without my knowledge."

Beatrice narrowed her eyes. "How did you know she was the one who broke in?"

"The lockpicks." His gaze drifted to the side. "They

were personalized—a gift from me a long time ago. At one point..." He shook his head. "It's not important."

"If you're not responsible for hiring Elise, then you have no idea what transpired here the other night," Giovanni said. "Take the journal and return it to Arosh. No vampire regent could find fault in you."

Giovanni knew he was only partly correct. Arosh was notoriously fickle. He could be forgiving or find fault for no reason at all. But that was what you signed on for when you worked for the Fire King.

"The play." Beatrice took a deep breath. "Shall we look?"

"Let's do it." With carefully washed hands, Giovanni gently set the book in a cradle before he opened it to the first page.

On the surface, it appeared to be exactly what it claimed, an eighteenth-century collection of one of the English Renaissance's most celebrated poets. There were pages of Jonson's poetry, a few essays, and then the plays started. *The Alchemist* was first, of course, but large chunks of the pages appeared to be missing.

"There's a gap in the binding," Beatrice murmured. "See there?"

"I do." Giovanni carefully lifted the pages and moved them from right to left. "Another play. *Volpone.*"

"The Fox," Beatrice murmured. She reached out and put a hand on Giovanni's. "Wait, no. That's not the play."

He looked up. "What?"

"Look at the binding. Look at the paper."

The pages themselves were faded, and the ink was different from the rest of the book. On first glance, they appeared to be bound, but they weren't, and Giovanni gently eased first one bundle of paper, then another one, from the cracked and crumbling volume.

"They're handwritten." He felt his heart move slowly. "The ink, Beatrice."

"I know." She moved a lamp closer and saw the bulb flicker. "Damn it, we need better lighting."

"This is it?" René leaned in. "You have found it?"

"I believe we have." Giovanni looked up. "It's faded. It hasn't been stored well in centuries. There is mold damage, but with the correct lighting and perhaps some lenses to enhance the ink…"

Beatrice's hands were trembling. "The ink may be faded, but the handwriting…"

René pointed to a scribble on the top of one page. "Does that say what I think it does?"

Giovanni's eyes focused on the top of the page René was pointing to.

The words were written in soft brown from ink that had spent years fading and changing. The paper was stained and torn in places. The handwriting was sharply slanted to the left, and the lower letters looped gracefully below the hand-drawn lines. There were words crossed out and a few notes in the margins.

And in the corner of a thick bundle of handwritten pages was a clear and distinct phrase.

Loves labours wonne.

The bundle of priceless handwritten pages had been carefully packed into an acid-free box that Giovanni had brought from London, and the library was put back in order by midnight the following evening.

"So Lord Mortimer will keep his gold, I think," René mused as their feet crunched over the blanket of snow covering the gravel walkway, "and spend it to start his music school."

"A good use of treasure." Beatrice walked René to the edge of the Audley property where the Frenchman had called his own car service. "And maybe a distraction from heartbreak."

"More than once Emilie—*Elise*—has been the cause of that."

She watched him, his shallow breaths visible in the cold night. His collar was turned up and his hair was slightly mussed, but he still looked like a high fashion model. The man had ridiculous genes.

Did he harbor feelings for his former protégée? If he did, Beatrice suspected he would never admit it.

"So where will you go to avoid your brother-in-law?"

"I have my own ways of returning home. The cretin doesn't control the entire island." René held a box with Arosh's journal packed carefully inside. "So this is what you do? Find lost manuscripts and books?"

She shrugged. "Scrolls. Newspapers. Mostly things for immortals who have lost or misplaced them over the years. We found a photo album once. It was in the archives of a university in Cologne."

"Showing pictures of a vampire who hadn't changed in centuries?"

"I think it was more sentimental than anything else." She smiled. "No one was going to notice the resemblance with the photographs packed away like that."

"Hmm." The Frenchman looked thoughtful. "It's not a bad line of work."

"Usually not very violent, though occasionally we run into a challenge or two."

"Like unscrupulous humans and their vampire allies?"

Beatrice kicked at the blanket of snow covering the ground. "Well, that could be describing half our family, couldn't it?"

"Indeed." A car pulled to the side of the lane and flashed its lights. "And that is my driver, of course. Do say hello to Benjamin and Tenzin for me." He frowned a little. "Will Terrance kill her?"

"Elise?" Beatrice took a long breath and let it out slowly. "I don't know."

"I'm the one who brought her into our world, but I'm not the one who introduced her to the life."

"The life of crime?"

"She was born into it." He smirked. "And she's the best actress I've ever met."

"Also a survivor, I'm guessing."

"She is that." He nodded. "Yes."

"Then I doubt we've seen her end, René du Pont.

Clear your conscience." She took a step back toward the house. "At least in this case."

Snow started to fall, sparkling in the headlights of the car in the lane. It touched René's blond hair and dusted his shoulders.

"Au revoir, Madame De Novo." René gave her a deep nod. "It was a pleasure to work with you instead of against you. When you decide the fate of the play, I trust you will make it right."

"When we know if it's genuine, I'll be in touch. And if we decide to keep it for ourselves, we'll send you a fair percentage of the appraised value."

He smiled. "You won't keep it for yourself. At least not forever."

Beatrice knew the man was right. In her heart of hearts, she was still a librarian. "Good night, René. And happy holidays, whatever you celebrate."

He walked into the shadows and disappeared, the muffled sound of the car door shutting the only sign of him before the black sedan sped into the night.

"And away from England he speeds." Beatrice turned to the glowing lights of Audley Manor in the distance. Who was the villain here? The thief who came to steal what was stolen from another? The one who stole without knowing? Or the villain who valued ambition over innocent life?

"Will was right," she murmured into the cold night. "The devil is a definitely a gentleman."

Mystery and adventure made her blood flow, but the

night was as cold as the great stone manor house, and Beatrice was ready to go home.

T he fire rose in the night, sparks flying into the eucalyptus-scented air of San Marino. Ben and Dema stood nearby after they situated Caspar and Isadora on the porch and covered the elderly couple with blankets to ward off the cold.

Isadora's expression was bright, and she watched the girls. "Look at them. Kaya has gotten so tall. The little girls are growing up."

Caspar smiled. "That's what this is about, isn't it?"

"Do you think she should wait for her parents?"

Dema said, "The momentous occasion happened this morning, so she decided that this had to take place tonight." The nanny smiled at Isadora. "Since this is Sadia's thing, she gets to make the rules."

Caspar nodded. "Very appropriate."

The guest of honor stood next to the fire in her favorite shirt, the grey one with black crosses on it. Her best friend Kaya stood behind her, wearing a white shirt with grey crosses. Both girls wore a solemn expression as Tenzin and Zain added wood to the fire.

"Dark and light twins," Ben whispered to Dema.

The nanny nodded. "So cool."

"Much cooler than us."

With reverence, Tenzin flew into the air, holding a

gold vase. She reached inside, then brought her hand out, tossing water over Sadia, who stood before the fire with her arms outstretched. Then she threw some of the water into the fire where it steamed and rose in a cloud.

"Rainwater from the neighbor's catch barrels," Dema said.

"Rainwater?"

"Something about a storm goddess from Aleppo."

Ben nodded. "That's pretty cool."

"Tap water wasn't okay—it had to be rainwater, so I told her the Prescotts had a really big vegetable garden and probably had rain buckets."

"Good thinking."

"I have my moments."

Sadia sat on a leopard-skin rug as Tenzin landed behind her.

Dema asked, "Is that a real leopard skin?"

"Yeah," Ben said. "It was in her storage unit here. I'm pretty sure it's a few hundred years old, so I don't think it's illegal, and I can't get her to get rid of it. She said the leopard tried to eat her and it was a fair fight, so she's keeping it."

"I guess since it's already dead..." Dema shrugged.

"With Tenzin, you have to pick your battles, and this was a better choice than her stealing a live leopard."

"Would she be able to—?"

"With her, anything is possible."

Tenzin was singing something low and droning, a hypnotic chant as she sat behind Sadia, who sat on the leopard skin before the fire, her hair damp from the rainwater. Steam rose from her hair as Tenzin motioned Ben and Dema over.

"You all have your gifts?" Tenzin asked.

The storm goddess Ḥepat was associated with many things, but her supplicants historically honored her with gifts of gold and silver, so Tenzin had asked Dema, Ben, and Zain for gifts of those two precious metals for Sadia on her initiation.

Caspar and Isadora asked Sadia if she could wait for a Christmas present and she told them that was fine.

Kaya raised her hand. "Wait, can I go first? I got her something too."

Sadia's face lit up. "You did?"

Kaya nodded enthusiastically as she reached into her pocket.

Sadia gleefully opened a small silk bag. "I love it!"

"It's a real silver bracelet," Kaya said. "My mom helped me pick it out yesterday. Look." She pointed. "It has two hands on it. For us."

"I love it." Sadia held it to her heart, then immediately put it around her wrist. "Thank you, Kaya."

Dema stepped up next. "I had planned to wait to give this to you, but I think Tenzin is right. Now is the perfect time." She held out a small box and looked on as Sadia opened it. "The cross is the traditional symbol of the Syriac Orthodox Church where you were baptized as an infant."

Sadia looked up with glistening eyes. "In the picture of my parents that I have, my mother is wearing one just like this."

Dema smiled. "I know. I had one made that was just like hers."

Sadia swallowed hard and stood to give Dema a hug. "Can you put it on me?"

"Of course." She carefully draped the necklace around Sadia's neck and closed the clasp. "It might be a little bit long now, but remember, you're still growing."

Sadia's face lit up as she touched the cross. "It's perfect. Thank you." She returned to her seated position on the leopard-skin rug. She grinned at Tenzin. "This is so cool."

Tenzin gestured to Sadia. "This was your idea. I only helped."

Zain stepped forward and knelt beside Sadia. "I know I'm not technically family," he said solemnly, "so I want to thank you for inviting me to this. I am honored."

Sadia's eyes went wide. "Of course you're family."

The man's brown eyes creased in the corners. "Then this is the perfect time to give you *this*." He handed her a small box.

Sadia tore into the beautifully wrapped square box.

"You know my family's from the South," Zain continued. "And all my sisters and cousins got these when they made their debut. My grandma and grandpa are old-fashioned like that."

Sadia opened the box, and Ben saw a silver charm bracelet inside. "It's so pretty."

"It has your initials on there," Zain said. "It's old-school, I know, but as you get older, you can add things to make it more personal for you."

Sadia looked into Zain's eyes. "This is really great. Thank you. And tell your mom and dad I said thank you too."

"I definitely will." He kissed the top of her head and stood up, nodding at Ben. "You're up, big bro."

Ben sat down beside his baby sister and took a moment to look at her.

The curves of her baby cheeks were fading away, and her face was stretching out. Her legs were coltish like a growing foal. Her cheekbones were more angular, and in the shadows cast by the fire, he could see the planes of the face she would wear as a woman.

He touched her chin and angled it toward him. "You're growing up."

Her cheeks reddened a little. "Yeah."

"I'm really proud to be your big brother." He looked at Tenzin. "We're both really proud of the person you're becoming."

Her embarrassed smile fell. "Thanks."

"You know, I thought this was kind of a weird idea when Tenzin first brought it up."

Sadia rolled her eyes. "I'm so shocked."

Ben smiled. "But now I think it's a great idea."

Her eyes turned mischievous. "Are you, like, trying to get your own initiation ceremony because you missed out when you were thirteen and didn't get any presents?"

Kaya giggled, and Ben heard Dema laugh too.

Ben looked at Tenzin. "That's it; no more school. She's going to be smarter than us if she keeps going."

"Too late now," Tenzin said.

"Yes!" Sadia threw her arms up. "No more school!"

Dema cleared her throat. "I don't think Ben gets to make that decision."

Sadia groaned, and Ben took the opportunity to place her gift in her lap.

"This is from me and Tenzin," he said. "Well, I picked it out, but it's from her treasure cache."

Sadia blinked innocently. "'Cause she has better stuff than you?"

Zain snorted.

"I mean, do you *want* an antique silver sextant?" He reached for the box. "Because I have an extra one lying around if you'd rather—"

"This is fine!" Sadia smiled as she opened the carved rosewood box, but then her eyes froze on what was inside and her mouth dropped open. "Ben, this is way too fancy."

"You save it for when you're older, okay?" He reached over and lifted it. "For tonight though, it can sit next to your cross."

The piece that he'd picked out was a Scythian gold torque from the third century. It was a thick crescent of pure gold with a delicate series of chains hanging in back. Tiny twisting depictions of animals, flowers, and mythical figures decorated the front, and gemstones hung from the chains in the back.

"I received this as payment for the very first treasure-hunting job that Tenzin and I did in China." He reached behind her neck and affixed the clasp of the torque. "This was my fee for driving a really stinky vegetable truck all the way across the country."

Tenzin said, "And I originally acquired it in Russia a very long time ago."

"For real?" Sadia turned to Kaya. "Look at this."

Wearing ancient gold around her neck, Sadia looked like a young queen.

Kaya's eyes were the size of saucers. "That is so cool."

"It's a grown-up present," Ben said. "But you're growing up. So" —he glanced at Tenzin— "this can be your first piece of treasure in your hoard, little dragon."

Her eyes were wide, and her fingers pressed against the gold at her neck. "I think this is too much."

Ben shook his head. "Nope. It's not. But after tonight, we'll put it in the safe until you're older, okay?"

She smiled, her expression relaxing with relief. "Okay."

Sadia jumped up and stood, gold at her neck and silver around her wrists. She turned her face to the fire with a defiant expression. "My name is Sadia. I was born during a war, and my first parents gave me my first name. My second parents gave me my second name. And tonight I'm choosing my third name. Hayat. Because I'm alive."

Sadia Isadora Hayat. It was a strong name, one worthy of the girl who had survived a war and a near-fatal migration to safety.

Caspar and Isadora clapped, and Ben stood watching his sister as she danced around the fire with her friend, the girls laughing and whooping in the darkness as the sparks flew higher in the cool night air.

"This was such a great idea," he said.

Dema and Zain flanked him.

"Agreed," Dema said.

"Makes me wish I got more than a lecture about personal hygiene from my dad on my thirteenth birthday," Zain said. "He did give me a bottle of Old Spice though."

Dema snorted.

Tenzin walked out from behind the house, holding a brown-and-white calf with a rope around its neck.

Ben looked at her, then at the cow. "Absolutely not."

Tenzin frowned. "It's traditional to honor the goddess Ḥepat with gifts of cattle, and your sister already said she didn't want to slaughter a goat."

Ben looked at Sadia, who had stopped when she heard the first moo.

The girl's eyes went wide, and then her mouth dropped open in delight. "Tenzin, you got me a *cow*?"

FIFTEEN

When Beatrice walked through the door of her home in San Marino, the first thing she noticed was the smell of tamales and the sound of Christmas pop playing in the kitchen.

"Hey, everyone."

Zain and Isadora looked up from the table where they were spreading masa on softened corn husks.

"B!" Zain hopped up to greet her.

"Oh!" Isadora smiled widely. "You're home early. Where's Giovanni?"

"Talking with security." They had arrived in the afternoon but had to wait until nightfall to leave the plane hangar. "Is Sadia—?"

"Mom!" Sadia came barreling into the kitchen from the living room. "Tenzin said she smelled you!"

And Beatrice knew the minute she saw her daughter that she'd missed something important. "Sadia! You—"

Sadia slapped a hand over her mouth. "Everyone knows already, but we don't have to talk about it."

"Oh sweetie." Beatrice hugged her daughter. "I'm sorry I wasn't here."

"It's cool. Tenzin was here."

Beatrice switched to Arabic, which neither Isadora nor Zain spoke. "And you have everything you need?"

"Mama, don't worry, I'm fine. It's no big deal." Her cheeks were red, but she switched back to English. "Did you have a good time in England? Did you find the thing you were looking for?"

Beatrice smiled and let her go even though she wanted to hold on a little longer. "We did. Dad has it packed away. It's a very old manuscript that we think was written by Shakespeare himself."

"What?" Zain's eyes went wide. "That's amazing."

"No way." Sadia slid beside Isadora and started helping with the tamales. "That's so cool, Mom. You and Dad have the coolest job ever."

Beatrice blinked. What had happened to her moody daughter who thought nothing and no one over the age of eighteen—other than Zain of course—was cool? "Thanks. We're pretty excited about it."

Zain asked, "You run into any trouble while you were looking for it?"

She smiled. "Nothing we couldn't handle. Met up with some old friends. Spent ages in a giant library."

"That sounds like fun." Sadia handed a corn husk to Isadora. "We had a bonfire last night."

"Oh yeah? That sounds fun too."

Her daughter's eyes sparkled with secrets. "It was really fun. Kaya came over, and then tonight Isadora said that since Christmas is next week, we needed to start the tamales."

"Your great-grandmother is wise." Beatrice slid onto the bench against the wall, sandwiching Sadia between her mother and her great-grandmother. "Is that a new necklace?" She saw the gold peeking from Sadia's black T-shirt. "That's beautiful."

Sadia looked up, and Beatrice knew there was a story that she wasn't getting. "Uh, yeah. Early Christmas present from Dema."

"It's beautiful." She looked at her grandmother.

I'll tell you later. Isadora's eyes spoke volumes.

"Well good," Beatrice said. "Sounds like you had a great time."

Sadia leaned her head against Beatrice's arm for a moment. "Missed you."

And her heart melted. "Missed you too, honey."

Giovanni was overseeing the unloading of their luggage when Ben wandered over.

Giovanni smiled. "There you are. I was wondering why everyone was hiding inside."

"Tamale-construction night."

"Ah." He gave Ben a quick embrace. "That definitely explains it."

"How was England?"

"Cold." Giovanni looked toward the south lawn. "Do I smell woodsmoke?"

"Sadia's friend came over last night and we did a bonfire."

"A bonfire when it's sixty degrees at night," Giovanni muttered. "She's definitely a Southern California girl."

"No worries around here. Smooth sailing," Ben said.

The man was hiding something, but Giovanni would find out eventually. "Good. We had a little fun in England looking for the play."

Ben's eyebrows went up. "Fun?"

"Your aunt ninja-stalked a group of thieves breaking into the manor house where we were searching for the manuscript, and then the thieves took hostages and they all ended up getting locked into a vault while I was in London. Nobody died, and we turned the thieves over to the authorities."

Ben blinked. "Well, that's an unexpected twist."

"I guess Beatrice had more fun than I did." He patted Ben on the shoulder and started for the kitchen, grabbing the briefcase with the manuscript on the way. "Oh! René du Pont sends his regards."

"René?" Ben scowled. "Guess I should have been expecting that when you said there were thieves in the library."

"Oh no," Giovanni said. "This time he was helping us."

"He was... What?" Ben rushed to catch up with Giovanni. "What do you mean, he was helping?"

"In fact, we may actually owe him a favor."

"I'm sure they didn't intend to irritate you when they worked with the Frenchman." Tenzin patted Ben's thigh as they watched Sadia and Beatrice decorate the Christmas tree in the living room. "They were using the resources in front of them, and René can be very—"

"Can we not?" He felt like a sulking child, but he had so many questions, and both Giovanni and Beatrice seemed to enjoy dropping hints without telling him the whole story. "René isn't supposed to be in England. He's banned."

"Hard to ban a vampire completely," Tenzin said. "Technically, I'm not allowed in Thailand, but that hardly stops me from visiting, does it?"

Ben frowned. "Why would you be banned from— Never mind." He nodded at the tree. "Sadia seems happier."

"Of course she is." Tenzin curled into Ben's side. "She is loved and seen by the people most important to her. And when children are that age, absence *does* make the heart grow fonder. Of parents anyway."

He leaned over and kissed his mate's temple. "Why don't we stay through the holidays? We can head back east after the New Year."

"You want to spend more time with your sister."

"She's growing so fast." He frowned. "In a blink, she won't be a kid anymore."

Tenzin let out a contented sigh. "She has a good childhood. Much better than either of us."

Yes. Until Giovanni had found Ben, his childhood had been very different from Sadia's. "I want her to be strong, but I don't want her to *have* to be strong. Does that make sense?"

"Perfectly." She wove her fingers through his, lifted his knuckles to her lips, and kissed them. "We are what our pasts make us, but it's not wrong to want a softer life for those we love."

Ben wrapped his arms around her. "You're wonderful. You know that."

"I do know that. The fertility rite was an excellent idea."

"Please don't call it a fertility rite in front of Giovanni."

"Fine, but I'm not going to lie about the tattoo."

Damn it, he'd almost forgotten about the tattoo. "It's tiny, right?"

"Define *tiny*."

Maybe heading back to New York was a good idea after all.

Giovanni walked into the living room from the library. He looked like he was moments from catching fire with excitement. "Zain just finished scanning all the manuscript pages with the camera, so we'll be able to read it as soon as he creates a file."

"So exciting." Ben put on a big smile. "When is the authenticator coming?"

"Not until after the holidays. He's in Oxford until then." Giovanni walked over to Beatrice and took the ornament she handed him. "The tree looks wonderful."

"And the tamales are steaming right now." She lifted on her toes and gave him a kiss. "Can you go in the backyard and get more wood for the fireplace?"

"You realize that the air conditioner is on right now, correct?"

"I wanted a fire." She smiled. "Please?"

"Tesoro, all you need to do if you want a fire is—"

"Ew." Sadia covered her ears. "Ew, ew, ew. Don't be gross. Oh my God, you two are worse than Ben and Tenzin. Ew."

Giovanni laughed, then kissed his wife and leaned down to kiss his daughter on the top of her head. "Fine, I'll go get more wood for the completely unnecessary fire."

He walked out the french doors, and Sadia danced over to her phone and changed the music coming out of the speakers.

Moments later, Ben heard Giovanni yell from outside.

"Tenzin! Why is there a cow in my garden?"

EPILOGUE

Caspar paged through the printout of the play, already planning his reaction for the following night when Giovanni would ask his opinion.

"Oh dear." Isadora looked up, moving the reading glasses from her nose. "I'm not an expert but..."

He started to laugh. "It's really not very good, is it?"

Isadora's smile was painful. "They can always give it to Richard?"

Caspar's laugh grew. Richard Montegu was a famed actor of Shakespearean tragedy who'd been turned into a vampire against his will. His only outlet now was the touring theater company partially funded by Giovanni and Beatrice that performed exclusively at immortal events.

"It's a bit disappointing though, isn't it?" Isadora sighed. "Though I suppose every writer has their flops, don't they?"

"Flop?" He looked at the notes in the margins. "I don't think this was ever performed, my love."

She looked at the pages again. "There are stage notes though. See? Here in the margin."

"Feedback, I think. The writing is different." He pointed to one page. "Look at this one. 'Very terrible. No woman speaks like this.' Do you think...?"

Isadora's eyes lit up. "Perhaps Lady Penny's ancestor wasn't Shakespeare's lover but his editor? Maybe he gave it to her to read and she didn't like it, so he scrapped it and left the manuscript with her."

"It's possible."

She narrowed her eyes. "This play is... Well, it reminds me of *Much Ado about Nothing* a bit."

"Men returning from war to return to their loves they left behind?" Caspar nodded. "I definitely see the similarities."

"But the new Duke character... He's rather foul, isn't he?"

"*Taming of the Shrew.*" Caspar set down the pages. "That's what I was thinking. He reminds me of Petruchio from *Taming of the Shrew.*"

"Yes!" Isadora murmured, "Richard Burton really was so handsome, wasn't he?"

"Focus, darling." Caspar felt like he was young again, brainstorming with Giovanni on a new literary mystery. "Perhaps this play was an early draft and Shakespeare decided to remove that part of the plot and write it on its own."

"And after that, maybe he decided *not* to return to

Navarre after all. Maybe he decided that new characters were the better choice."

"Leave the King of Navarre with his ends and create a whole new cast of characters?"

"It's possible." Isadora set down the papers. "I enjoyed *Love's Labour's Lost*, but I never felt like it needed a sequel."

"Leave beloved characters to their imagined ends?" Caspar set the play aside and slid into bed next to his wife. "That's the writer's prerogative, I suppose."

"The audience can always use their imagination," Isadora said. "Not everything needs to be spelled out."

"I think there's a note like that in the margins somewhere." He turned off the bedside-table lamp. "I wonder what they'll do with this?"

"Even if the story isn't complete, it's still more than enough for Shakespeare fans to argue about, isn't it?"

"Very true." Caspar drew Isadora's head gently to his shoulder, where his wife's soft white hair tickled his nose.

He wouldn't end his nights in any other way.

"Good night, my darling."

"Good night, my love."

Happy Holidays!

November 20, 2024

Dearest readers,

I hope you enjoyed this holiday jaunt back to Giovanni and Beatrice Land. I had so much fun writing this, I'm seriously considering more literary mysteries with our favorite vampires.

So to all of you who have asked me over the years whether there will be more Giovanni and Beatrice books, I can only say to you...

Maybe?

Have a wonderful holiday season! I hope you're spending it with people you love, delicious food and drink, and more than a few good books to keep you company.

Happy holidays, and have a wonderful new year.

My best wishes to you and all your loved ones.

Sincerely,

Elizabeth Hunter

Whether you're a fan of contemporary fantasy, fantasy romance, or paranormal women's fiction, Elizabeth Hunter has a series for you.

THE ELEMENTAL MYSTERIES

Discover the series that has millions of vampire fans raving! Immortal book dealer Giovanni Vecchio thought he'd left the bloody world of vampire politics behind when he retired as an assassin, but a chance meeting at a university pulls student librarian Beatrice De Novo into his orbit. Now temptation lurks behind every dark corner as Vecchio's growing attachment to Beatrice competes with a series of clues that could lead to a library lost in time, and a powerful secret that could reshape the immortal world.

Ebook/Audiobook/Paperback

THE CAMBIO SPRINGS MYSTERIES

Welcome to the desert town of Cambio Springs where the water is cool, the summers sizzle, and all the residents wear fur, feathers, or snakeskin on full moon nights. In a world of cookie-cutter shifter romance, discover a series that has reviewers raving. Five friends find themselves at a crossroads in life; will the tangled ties of community and shared secrets be their salvation or their end?

Ebook/Audiobook/Paperback

THE IRIN CHRONICLES

"A brilliant and addictive romantic fantasy series." Hidden at the crossroads of the world, an ancient race battles to protect humanity, even as it dies from within. A photojournalist tumbles into a world of supernatural guardians protecting humanity from the predatory sons of fallen angels, but will Ava and Malachi's attraction to each other be their salvation or their undoing?

Ebook/Audiobook/Paperback

GLIMMER LAKE

Delightfully different paranormal women's fiction! Robin, Val, and Monica were average forty-something moms when a sudden accident leaves all three of them with psychic abilities they never could have predicted! Now all three are seeing things that belong in a fantasy novel, not their small mountain town. Ghosts, visions, omens of doom. These friends need to stick together if they're going to solve the mystery at the heart of Glimmer Lake.

Ebook/Audiobook/Paperback

And there's more! Please visit ElizabethHunter.com or sign up for her newsletter to read more about her work.

ACKNOWLEDGMENTS

Abundant thanks to all the readers who made writing this novella so enjoyable! I hope I have done justice to your love for these characters. A very happy holiday season from Beatrice and Giovanni, Sadia, Ben, and Tenzin.

And also from me.

Thanks to my wonderful editors Amy Cissell and Anne Victory. And special thanks to Linda for her encyclopedia-like expertise on British peerage systems.

Many thanks to my excellent agent, Kimberly Brower, and to my PR company, Valentine PR.

And finally, thanks to my husband for his love, support, and always remembering to make me eat when I forget. I love you so much.

ABOUT THE AUTHOR

ELIZABETH HUNTER is an eleven-time *USA Today* bestselling author of contemporary fantasy, paranormal romance, and paranormal mystery. Based in Central California and Addis Ababa, Ethiopia, she travels extensively to write fantasy fiction exploring world mythologies, history, and the universal bonds of love, friendship, and family. She has published over fifty works of fiction and sold over a million books worldwide. She is the author of the Elemental Mysteries universe, the Irin Chronicles, the Cambio Springs series, and other works of fiction.

ElizabethHunter.com

Also by Elizabeth Hunter

Shadows and Gold

Imitation and Alchemy

Omens and Artifacts

Midnight Labyrinth

Blood Apprentice

Night's Reckoning

Dawn Caravan

The Bone Scroll

Pearl Sky

Tin God (coming Summer 2024)

The Elemental Covenant

(Carwyn and Brigid)

Saint's Passage

Martyr's Promise

Paladin's Kiss

Bishop's Flight

Tin God (coming Summer 2024)

The Seba Segel

The Thirteenth Month

Child of Ashes (coming 2024)

The Gold Flower (coming 2025)

The Irin Chronicles

The Scribe

The Singer

The Secret

The Staff and the Blade

The Silent

The Storm

The Seeker

Mirror Obscure

Trouble Play

Contemporary Romance

The Genius and the Muse

7th and Main

INK

HOOKED

GRIT

SWEET

Linx & Bogie Mysteries

A Ghost in the Glamour

A Bogie in the Boat